The Road to Heancurld

John Zegers

Now a book for Debbie, one of the best,
When the music begins, she's full of fresh Zest!
Now I can only hope my book passes her test.
So no more writing, for me, I'll give it a rest!

— *John Zegers (Zege)*

ISBN 978-1-0980-5208-9 (paperback)
ISBN 978-1-0980-5209-6 (digital)

Copyright © 2020 by John Zegers

All rights reserved. No part of this publication may be reproduced, distributed, or transmitted in any form or by any means, including photocopying, recording, or other electronic or mechanical methods without the prior written permission of the publisher. For permission requests, solicit the publisher via the address below.

Christian Faith Publishing, Inc.
832 Park Avenue
Meadville, PA 16335
www.christianfaithpublishing.com

Printed in the United States of America

Contents

Acknowledgments 5
Introduction 7
Section 1:   Moordarey
        The Road to Heancurld 11
        Winawurld's Girl 14
        Bombil's Conquest 17
        Hilfinkle Geast 18
        Hilfinkel's Brother 19
        Twigby's Cat 20
        Turaloe's Bread 21
        A Better Day for Flayen Dorft 24
        Klutsgorn and the Two Thugs 27
        Heancurld Winter 31
        Voyage to the Pollen Nation 36
        Klindorn and Glengarth 40
Section 2:   Earth
        The Storyteller 57
        Birdland Bedlamb 61
        Sea Drudge 63
        The Droggy Brother 64
        Elephant Titus 65
        Bored to Tears 66
        Frank N. Sense and His Fantastic Sidewalk Sail 67
        The Opera Tuna Tea 82
        Desert Sands 85
        The Heir of Castle McCloor 86

Love Poem of a Cad 95
Birth of a Revelation 96
The Gift of Music 98
Corcoran's Night Before Christmas 100
The Guide 102
Sequoia's Secret Realm 103
The Trail of the Owl 105
The Lady of Pine Lake 108
The Dragon Named Too Much 112
Solitary beneath the Stars 114
The End or Beginning? 116

Acknowledgments

I would sincerely like to thank all of those responsible for bringing this book into fruition, fulfilling the role of scribe in my poem, "The Storyteller."

Fathers Warren Schoeppe and Frank Parker S. J. who molded me into a writer, my family who gave me all kinds of help and inspiration for my pieces, Al and Wally Van Camp (formerly of Porterville and now of Fresno), the Griesbach Family of Tulare, Judge Glenda Doan of Corcoran, Aaron and Caleb of Gomes of Tulare, and finally Julie Sheppard and Alaina of Christian Faith Publishing, who have provided the professional and caring assistance that have ultimately made this life's dream possible!

Introduction

Halloween themes tend to darken every year, *The Ghost of Castle McCloor* offers a delicious intriguing mystery set in an ancient Scottish castle with a fresh and novel twist. Nestled warmly in our collection are poems well suited for the season of Christmas, such as "Heancurld Winter" and more notably "A Gift of Music," drawn from the author's own family history. These selections prove equal enrichment for armchair or classroom environments.

The *Of Earth and Moordarey* collection reflects approximately forty years of its writer's written life experiences in the realms of spirit, nature, and family life, as well as numerous flights of unrestrained fancy.

The advantage of the poetic medium is that it is so amenable to the readers' time availability, as well as to his mood. We have already taken a looked at mood and tonal considerations, so let us now concentrate on our time benefits. If the reader wants to immerse himself or herself in a longer short story with more plot and character development, "Klindorn and Glengarth," a tale of kings and warriors, is made to order, whereas a selection like *The Ghost of Castle McCloor* reaches more of a middle ground. A more brief escape into that realm where mystic forces come to dance on a shore of natural splendor is to be found in our "Lady of Pine Lake."

Sometimes we have no time and even less patience. A quick pick-me-up is then in order. Most of us can relate to the genius and mirth of Ogden Nash and the staying power of his simple limericks. The reader would not be disappointed to find in our fair collection, no shortage of the quick yet satisfying in-and-out-type rhymes.

In this skeptical and overcrowded world, what this collection *Of Earth and Moordarey* needs is a publisher whose presentation will invite a casual shopper to take a closer look, to feel an invitation into a world that will refresh and entertain him or her for a brighter reentry into our own!

Section 1
Moordarey

The Road to Heancurld

There is a land beyond our own where our sun is but a star,
This place is a lovely planet which is so vastly far,
That you must stretch forth from the borders of your mind
If this land you seek to find.

Through a small corner of this distant world
Threads the road to Heancurld,
A tiny village of a tiny folk
That style themselves the Bimaroke.

Lining there, this rural path, stand the giant gilgoan trees,
Deep green, the leaves shade its bark as white as the winter freeze
Into three great branches, the foliage naturally weaves,
As do our clover or the Irish shamrock leaves.

And here the birds with a happy song
Chatter and soar the whole day long
Under the warmth of their brilliant sun
Dropping their refuse on anyone.

The gilgoan's branches are stripped to sticks
And form the fences stuck upright in bricks,
Allowing free vision to the countryside,
Since the gaps between are fairly wide.

The stocks of wheat are stunted but rich,
And with gentle breeze, the stocks do pitch,
While in reds and yellows, the fields now glow,
As the fragrant flowers present their show.

Blooms of yellow and blooms of blue,
Fill the hills and the valleys too.
Except where the fruit trees block the view,
And come to think of it, there are quite a few.

Oh, up on hills, the Bimaroke dwell.
Where they can see about their lands quite well,
Upon second-story porches built quite high,
For this is a curious people who love to spy.

But far are they from the Forongorth,
Those gallant axmen of the north,
Who sail their ships through the frigid sea
Where ice makes mountains for men to see.

Uniting and protecting all nations and lands
From their wooded homeland to the desert sands,
Building their ships and conducting their trade,
They protect that land from those who invade.

Tall and strong and fair of skin
Is the average among these men
Though not so advanced in some degree
As either the Vladyos or Kulu Chee.

But please forgive me, I've wandered astray,
For you see it was the only way
In which I could give you a glimpse or clue
That other races live here too.

But we were traveling the road to Heancurld,
So let us join young Duur and Winawurld,
Two Bimaroke friends on their way to town,
Dressed in working clothes of green and brown.

Around the bend into the square, they walked
And looked to the village of varied rock,
Where all of the shops and even the square
Are built of stone with precision care.

And all the shops are built low you see,
To allow the sun its shining glee.
And the shopkeepers' houses line surrounding hill,
For to snoop into town, for them, is a thrill.

And so the road to Heancurld
Is but a fragment of that world,
Which lies in a galaxy far away,
On the distant planet called Moordarey.

Winawurld's Girl

Solemnly sat Winawurld wishing away
That he might see his love before the end of the day,
With her eyes that were flashing to make him quite gay.
The boy had it bad; it was needless to say!

Her laugh was the sunshine that frightens the chill,
To do without her was making him ill.
For in her red dress dancing, his mind saw her still,
That void in his heart, she was perfect to fill.

But alas and alack and great heart attack!
She was the daughter of none but old Waldaclack,
Who could bust a post with but one mighty wack
And would be glad to put a crack in his back.

Although Winawurld's heart felt as big as a plum,
That little Bimaroke youth wasn't that dumb.
He had no desire to be smashed like a crumb.
He'd lost most of his sense, but he still had some.

Old Waldaclack's fists were of nectarines size,
And his muscles like duck eggs would flex with surprise,
No man would sit when fire reached his eyes,
For no one was safe when his anger did rise.

But his daughter, Elemur, was quite lovely, it's true.
Though she'd inherited that temper less hot than a few,
But this was no cause to make Winawurld stew,
For his temper was shorter than his size too.

But less strong than his temper was the fear that he had,
And how he wished to dispose of her despicable dad.
So poor Winawurld was in a state that was sad,
Like was once said before, he had it quite bad.

The only course open was to grab her and flee
To a place where they could live in peace happily.
But in his mind, old Waldaclack, he could still see,
Seizing him roughly and breaking him over his knee.

The heart of Winawurld was brave and quite true;
A Bimaroke must do what a Bimaroke must do.
If his love he wished to successfully pursue,
He would take whatever risk his fate would ensue.

So to Waldaclack's cottage he did stealthfully sneak.
Each step that he took made him less brave and more meek.
His hands were ice cold, and his knees were quite weak,
And he wondered if he could trust his voice true to speak.

Cold feet had risen to his neck and his head.
He hoped in the morrow, he wouldn't be dead,
But sharing a life with his love in its stead.
She had stolen his heart gaily dancing in red.

Reaching Waldaclack's cottage, he sighed with delight,
For that miserable tyrant was nowhere in sight.
His face was now happy; his step was quite light.
He'd take his fair beauty without threat of a fight.

There on the low porch, cracking fresh nuts sat she,
Filling our hero's heart with such glee,
That he jumped from behind the old gilgoan tree,
Failing her father's dread shadow to see!

Approaching her quickly, his advance was cut short
When he heard the horrid Waldaclack snort
And realized too late, it was no time to court,
So he trembled there bravely, his thoughts trying to sort.

There stood Waldaclack his mouth changing shapes,
His eyes were the size of fat purple grapes,
With his black beard a glistening like the demons' foul capes,
And Winawurld could think of no daring escapes!

"Marry or bury!" cried Waldaclack gruff,
"Or for disturbing my daughter, I'll give you a cuff.
I've been watching your antics, and I'm tired of that stuff."
So the decision of our hero wasn't really that tough.

Bombil's Conquest

Young Bombil sought the baker's daughter.
The fair and lovely Teralawter,
After tries and trials, he finally caught her
And married her soon as he thought he oughter,
Then for the rest of his life, he daily fought her,
But he was the victim of the slaughter.

Hilfinkle Geast

In Heancurld was a wedding feast!
Which pleased the greatest and the least,
But most of all Hilfinkle Geast,
Who was twice as fat as the dinner beast!

No gift had he for bride and groom,
But to fill in his belly the empty room,
He quick to the hall did readily zoom,
And wondered Hilfinkle, who married whom!

Hilfinkel's Brother

Hilfinkel Geast had a brother thin,
Who hated to admit Hilfinkel was kin,
But still his brother, Hilfinkel, came in
And emptied his table again and again.

Twigby's Cat

Twigby Tibler the Bimaroke sat
By the hearth of stone and watched his cat,
Deciding there the cat was fat.
Quite pleased was Twigby concerning that
Since in her belly rested a rat!
This was no animal he wished to scat,
Or chase out the door with his Bimaroke hat,
For she had earned her place on Twigby's mat!

Turaloe's Bread

Twigby Tibler's talented wife
Baked fine bread all of her life
And all craved a slice cut by her knife,
But her daughter's bread caused intestinal strife!

Poor Twigby then would feel quite low,
When the baking urge would hit sweet Turaloe,
For the manner in which she would knead her dough
Could strangle to death a full grown crow!

Well, into town, there staggered a bum,
Who at the Tibler cottage begged for a crumb,
Quite ignorant of the disaster to come,
For sweet Turaloe was quick to give some!

Now to ask for food was but part of his deal,
For this ragged beggar desired more than a meal,
Of Bimarove bread and a slice of cold veal.
This wretched fellow had come in to steal!

Into the house, he came with a bound!
And he began to look around and around,
Evaluating closely each object he found,
Desiring to add to his treasure mound!

"It is kind of you to do me this turn,"
Said the thief with a bow, feigning concern,
Before sampling the morsel that would make his gut churn.
T'was a matter of minutes before he would learn.

Sitting down promptly, a plan he did make,
Of all the things he decided to take,
And as he did this, our unsuspecting ole fake,
Ate some of the bread that Turaloe did bake!

Then stood tall the robber, Tyron Drife,
Reaching deep in his pocket for his threatening knife,
But just at that moment, he began his own strife!
Choking, he begged Turaloe to save his own life!

Tyron then went into a terrible fit!
Coughing and gagging, he tried hard to spit,
Puzzling Turaloe from where she did sit,
And angry she grew for she thought it was wit!

"Everyone here makes fun of my bread!
The boys in the village sent you here to get fed,
To tease, and to taunt me and play tricks in their stead!"
So yelling this loudly, she bashed in his head!

Then she looked up and the door; it crashed down!
For there stood Twigby with a grim fatherly frown,
Followed by neighbors who stood all around,
As word of this, Tyron had just reached their town.

Words of praise had they all for this heroine fair!
And a reward was hers when they discovered his lair,
(After removing the bread that had blocked off his air,
Turning him blue in his justifiable scare!)

In a fortnight or so, sweet Turaloe wed,
And produced a fine pair of sons, it was said!
For their mother's baking, they were never fed,
But they always grew full on their grandmother's bread!

A Better Day for Flayen Dorft

There on the border of Heancurld, the Bimaroke children were playing.
As the sun shone bright with a yellow light and the branches of the trees were swaying,
When once again, they saw Flayen Dorft, who had one extra finger.
And Flayen hurried past the group, for he didn't want to linger.

The children of Heancurld would mock and laugh at his deformed hand,
Which made it quite hard for him, as you can understand.
But to the children of Heancurld, it was a great delight
To laugh so hard and ridicule that quite unusual sight.

But down the road came old Bradiman,
One of the twelve great Gilgoads, a good and holy man,
Who saw this sight, both in anger and in pity.
And he sought to heal the wound in his manner, wild and witty.

He said, "I see before my eyes a very stupid band,
And yet another lad with an extra finger on his hand,
But my pity goes not with the boy but with this group instead.
For he is the only one I see with a normal head."

They looked to see the old man. In his old eyes, there dawned a twinkle.
And even they could understand, he had knowledge for every wrinkle.
He was one who walked with Him when He visited Moordarey.
With Him who came and left one day after teaching them the way.

He was a Bimaroke in his heart with no use for pretty speeches
But had an undying faith that humor better teaches.
He would delight to twist a word around till it bit its own behind
And twist it back again or let itself unwind.

Thus, he delivered to them all a clever speech.
So that he could preach awhile in a manner to constructively teach,
As well as keep the rising heat down on this summer's day.
By diverting the hot air cleverly in his uniquely Bimaroke way.

Then staring them all quite square in the face,
He doubled around and began to pace.
Old Bradiman knew just what he would say,
But he wished to annoy them with this useless delay.

"Everyone is a weirdo whom you know or I know,
Even if the strangeness isn't where it does show,
For some are weak and foolish inside
So that their weirdness is easy to hide.

"Their courage is false and so is their pride.
On the pain of their victims, they must take a ride.
They can't stand the thought that others might see,
That they themselves aren't as perfect as perfect can be!

"But each man is a world with strange lands in his mind.
No two the same, each one—one of a kind,
But a fool sees nothing but the difference between,
And he strikes like an animal that fears what he's seen.

"Learn to see with your mind, as well as your eyes,
And the world will shed its dark disguise,
So that you may know the truths from the lies
Know these things, and you'll grow to be wise."

Most of them listened to the words he had said.
Some of them shuffled and turned kind of red.
But Dilian Smutnik stood and laughed there instead.
"It sounds like the stories we're told before bed.

"I see a finger too many with both my eyes and my mind.
Any way I look, the spare finger I find!"
The others first smiled then shot a cold frown
At Dilian Smutnik, that drip of a clown.

But even with that, Bradirnan could see on his face,
That with Dilian Smutnik, he was getting no place.
But the old one knew his message might never travel across.
Although four out of five wasn't such a great loss.

For the old man knew that some listen and some don't,
That some like to hurt while others just won't.
But things got much better for Flayen that day,
So happily Bradiman went on his own way!

Klutsgorn and the Two Thugs

Throughout the south of Bimarove, the warning was sent out.
That a dangerous pair of criminals was roving there about!
Gilroab and Sunidan had leapt the prison's wall,
And all about the people watched, lest into their hands, they'd fall!

The duo was both of Bimaroke stock but strong for their own race.
T'was said the mess they left, when they robbed a place,
Was surely their mother's most bitter disgrace,
Along with their inheritance of a black sheep's roguish face.

The sloppy pair's great preference was to maul or kill.
A survey of their handiwork would surely turn you ill!
This service they rendered, for a price, if quite fully paid,
But should their provider shirk a bit, they'd share with him the blade.

Along the way to Heancurld, these motley maggots flew,
Doing along the way what motley maggots do,
Until they cast their dirty eyes (they couldn't use Murine),
Upon the home of Klutsgorn Slaak, a quiet lovely scene.

Now Klutsgorn Slaak was a man of apparent wealth,
Which could have proven hazardous to this good chap's health,
For the evil twain fully approved of this splendid view,
Perhaps, I'd say, even more than would I or maybe you.

Then Klutsgorn Slaak spied the pair, as to his house they neared,
And he welcomed them both cheerfully as men he'd long revered.
"I know who you are, my skillful guests and I hoped you'd choose my door.
My horrid brothers, I *have* for you a profitable little chore!"

The two grim brothers were taken back by this greeting gay,
And so they listened curiously on to what he had to say.
"In Bimarove, you're wanted men, in danger to be sure,
But if you do just what I say, your way will be secure!"

"And money, sir?" asked Sunidan with an evil smile.
Responded Slaak, "One thousand skels should last a little while."
"But a thousand skels is little pay for work done by our hand."
"A thousand skels is not just all, but freedom from this land!"

The brothers knew the heat was on, and this deal was quite ideal,
So they decided to do some honest work rather than to steal.
"I am married to a lovely wife and would never have another,
In fact, her greatest fault is her kinship to her mother!

"For ten good years, I lived at ease with my children and my wife,
But then that hag came to stay and ruin our good life.
You see, when her husband's life, in this world was spent,
The poor old thing was left alone with no one to torment!

"I ask you not to be too rough, for she's the mother of my wife.
Just end her life quite mercifully with a sharpened knife.
For I hear if the blade is dull, it can last a little while,
And I won't be responsible for murder of that style.

"My wife and kids will be away today for quite a length of time.
It really is a perfect day to perpetrate the crime!
Now come on in and have a meal for she sets a wondrous table,
But you'll likely find a lovelier beast in the pen behind the stable!"

So they walked into the house to her kindly greeting,
In fact, it was so loud and shrill; they bound her before eating
And watched her as she strained and squirmed in a frantic fury.
It was quite amusing since they didn't have a worry.

"Wife's Mother Dear, let me make it clear, you are charming with that gag,
But even so, I'll have you know, you are a hideous hateful hag.
I think I have a wonderful plan, but I really shouldn't brag.
Anyway I'll be rid of you, you fat and toothless bag!"

The other two liked the jest and laughed a little bit,
But the old woman shook herself in a frenzy of a fit.
And they were glad that she was tightly bound and not up raging free,
For she was quite a tough customer as anyone could see!

But still Klutsgorn continued on with the morbid joke
And set the three laughing so, they all began to choke.
"Now I'll grab some wine so we can drink to your due demise,
But I can't remove your gag, my dear, it wouldn't be too wise."

So up he sprang and grabbed the wine, the most excellent of hosts
And had them raise their glasses high for a little toast.
"To my mother-in-law, Manalu, may her long life be long enough."
So saying this quite gaily, he belted down the stuff.

Soon the brothers began to sway from the wine they drank.
Then the two began to rise, but to the floor, they sank,
For you see clever Klutsgorn had mickied the criminals' wine.
And this crystal sparkling brew did the job quite fine.

He immediately cut one hand free and left the lady the knife
And took off running toward the town to save his own dear life.
He had no fear of the peaceful thugs, lying sprawled out on the floor,
But his wife's gray-haired mother might want to even up the score!

He returned shortly thereafter with police from nearby town
And tried to calm the "dear old dame" to remove her deep set frown.
"I didn't mean those dirt mean things that I so despicably said,
But I'd rather hurl you insults than to see us both stabbed dead!

"When I saw those terrible hoods, there was nothing more to do
But pretend that I wanted them to slaughter off dear you.
I'll be more than glad to split with you, the reward for each bad guy!"
Then the charming lady punched him smack straight in the eye!

Heancurld Winter

The winter snows above Heancurld began to dance about,
Falling blue and landing white the roads and fields they covered,
And all the vestiges of fall's last dance season were slowly blotted out,
As winter's birth was blossomed forth while above, the snow clouds hovered.

The old folks sighed to see the sight, already their bones were aching.
But the children laughed with pure delight, for God made snow for playing.
Soon they'd turn back to their homes where there was hot bread baking,
And all the folks both young and old knew that winter was staying.

The wheels went off from the Bimaroke carts to be stored for drier season.
The skis went on in their place as runners for the snow.
And the harness beasts the skickaroe began to howl without apparent reason,
For snowy days mean colder feet, these faithful servants know.

The skickaroe are splendid beasts of a canine class.
Large and black with bright-red tongues, they make a ferocious sight,
Like great black wolves with reflective eyes, almost like a looking glass.
They are gentle and obedient, yet loyal in a fight.

For saddle or for pulling loads, they are a handy friend,
Serving as beast and guardian there over the Bimaroke land.
The little children they keep from harm and all the stock defend,
Fulfilling faithfully, all loving owners demand.

There in the tavern, Laughing Sun, the fire is blazing bright,
As the young and old gather there for the evening's rest,
Where they can drink and talk and sing far into the night.
And old man, Rigiborg, greets with cheer each familiar guest.

In the east corner, the players play a merry song,
As old men talk of crops and things they did when they were young.
The younger folks sit in-their groups, sometimes staying a bit too long,
Refusing to relinquish their fun until the last song was sung.

At his place, old Twigby sits chewing his smiderow
(Which is much like our tobacco, it's useful to chew or smoke)
As he stared out in to the night to catch the winter snow,
Only passing to smile and laugh at some familiar joke.

Rigiborg's cat is resting fine near the roaring blaze,
Where he sleeps behind the hearth, there where the woodbox sits.
And when it raises its old head up, half in a sleepy daze,
Old Twigby nails it in the eye with his smiderow spits.

And his thoughts reached back to the year before when the ice hard
    froze,
When he took his grandsons out to fish on the icy brook.
He felt all the time the chill that reddened his nose
As he inspected carefully the line and then the hook.

After the two had begun, the grandfather decided to say,
"If you build a fire by the icy hole, you'll be able to catch more fish,
For they'll swim toward the fire to warm themselves on such a cold
    bleak day."
So with his help, they accomplished his task to achieve their fishy wish.

This being done, Twigby stepped back as the fire did glow.
And the warmth that it made took the chill from the wintry ice.
Appearing as a yellow light upon the glistening snow,
As Twigby watched with a crackling grin, thinking to himself, *How nice.*

And soon that ice so white was beneath the water blue,
As were the knees of those grandsons too,
So cold, they ran to Twigby straight, asking dear grandfather what to do.
Though they knew by now his words weren't always true.

Cackling and chuckling wickedly, he returned the skin-soaked pair,
And quickly, he left before their story of treachery was told,
Waiting a few days cautiously before going back over there,
For his daughter, Turaloe, knew well how to scold.

When he arrived, he discovered the two were lying snug in bed.
It seems they had each contracted a terrible sniffly cold.
Each one was suffering from a mucous-filled head,
So into his cagey mind, a new idea rolled.

"For a fisherman's cold, there can be only one sure cure—
You must eat a raw fish, slick and fat, like the ones here in my bag,
If you want to get better quick, it's the best way to be sure!
I know a lot about medicine, but I don't like to brag."

They stared for a while uneasily at the cold raw fish,
Their eyes and their stomachs in perfect harmony, rolling just as one,
As they picked their cure reluctantly from the blue-colored dish,
While Twigby fought laughter back from his newfound fun.

A couple of bites were all that each could take,
Before their stomachs jumped about like a startled frog,
And Grandfather Twigby with mean delight and laughter then did shake,
But on the sun of his merriment descended a heavy fog.

Angry young Turaloe stood glaring at the door,
And poor old Twigby Tibler was laughing then no more!
He shuffled his feet sheepishly against the hard stone floor,
Waiting for his daughter to even up the score.

She raged, and she shrieked like a banchee from the pits of hell,
Until he promised her soup meat and a hand-carved chair.
Like his grandsons at that time he was feeling none too well,
When he like a Daniel left saved from danger's lair.

The sparks of these thoughts danced in his mind with the crackling
    fire,
As his son and son-in-law paced to where he sat,
And he knew to return home was now their desire.
Yes, old Twigby himself had no objections to doing that.

The three wives were gathered at Twigby's house that night
To discuss family talk and all the Bimaroke chatter,
About who visited who and the neighbor's big fight
And other things, that don't really matter.

The grandchildren would be asleep on the wooden floor,
Where they tried to stay awake to hear just a little bit more,
So the chatter would continue amidst an occasional snore,
All of this, Twigby knew well, as he walked toward the tavern door.

He grumbled and cussed at the foul weather outside,
As the three made their way through the chill of the snow.
Climbing into the sleigh wagon, over the white they did ride,
Bundled up tightly they were, all huddled down quite low.

As Twigby's cottage came welcomely into their plain view,
The skickaroe were barking eagerly and fanning their wide tails.
The animals were happy, and the Bimaroke were too,
For all of them knew it signaled the end of their frigid trails.

Glingore, his son, opened wide the heavy barn room door,
And the wagon rolled right in as it had always done before,
Into the stone barn, resting on the solid ground floor.
They then unharnessed the creatures—making sure they weren't sore.

So then up the stairs, the three men strode,
To the kitchen-living room where the bright fire burned,
And the chatter of the gossip incessantly flowed,
Yes, where the three could discover what their dear wives had learned.

The younger people decided the time was growing late,
So gathering their children, they talked a bit more.
Saying goodbye several times, then deciding again to stay,
Taking about an hour before, they made it out the housedoor.

So the two senior Tiblers went back up for a while,
To sit and grow sleepy watching the skipping fire,
And make occasional comments in their same old style.
The heat of the room grew too much which caused them to perspire.

She complained of his habits, which she found most uncouth.
And he remarked, as most always, she was getting too fat,
As he spewed some smiderow from his half-broken tooth,
So they continued in like manner with this or maybe with that.

When sleep began to rock them gently away,
They trod down the stairs to the cold bedroom below,
Where they would wake to a new winter's day,
And such is a typical day of the Heancurld snow.

Voyage to the Pollen Nation

Young Dallion Stall sat all day long and dreamed of the Pollen Nation,
Where breezes blow from dusk till dawn with little hesitation.
Upon his walls sat landscapes drawn filled by various vegetation,
And blooms pale and bloom bright, singing the glory of God's creation!
Until his father cried, "Get up, my boy!" to stifle his imagination.

Though he labored through his life quite drear,
Those distant isles were ever near,
The haunting cries of free birds he'd hear,
Until from his image ship would those shores appear!

Dallion's worried family would nag our lad,
While the neighbors said, "Well, it's just too bad!"
Or "Don't notice it's just a young man's fad."
But the dauntless Dallion held as fast as he had!

The years could not hide the image inside,
Of these islands of life so fair and so wide.
On the wings of a seabird, he'd soar and then glide!
His driving desire would not be denied!

On a day so darn hot that you'd swear you could roast,
There came into the shop a man from the coast.
He told of adventures and, Lord, how he'd boast,
And he offered young Dallion what he'd dreamed most!

Before dark fled the morning, Dallion said his goodbye,
Before the sun said, "Awaken!" from his throne in the sky!
They crossed the wide valley before climbing on high,
Then down coastal mountains where the ocean birds cry!

They found work on a ship, docked at the great port,
And his friend helped school him in work of that sort,
Which was dangerous and difficult, he'd latter report,
Leaving him surprised at the lengths to which he'd resort!

T'was on the day he'd nearly fallen and broken his neck,
When the ship had pitched him from the mast toward the deck,
As it rammed the submerged hull of a wreck,
Run a ground in the shadow of Mt. Eck!

Dallion starred from the rail, there to find,
Images in reality he'd first seen in his mind,
Of fish, birds, and fauna of every color and kind!
He blessed the day he'd left his homeland behind!

They'd seen their destination, but that was not all
To be deposited at the Pollen Nations first port of call,
Being loaded into a canoe that would pitch and then fall,
Spidering down a rope ladder at barely a crawl!

Dallion waved back to his mates and turned, welcoming his fate.
Gone were those years he just had to wait!
His rowers proceeding at a quick, steady rate,
His heart keeping time with his emotional state!

The Pollen Nation was truly a sight to behold,
White diamond coasts and vegetation untold,
Swaying palms giving shade to blossoms of pure gold,
Cooled by tropical breezes, never grew quite cold!

Dallion was escorted by men smiling and built strong,
Who introduced him to sisters before very long.
Their voices soft and sweet mingled with birds in their song!
What in this paradise could possibly go wrong?

In less than three days, the wind shifted in its way.
It could be seen in the water and how the trees did sway,
And Dallion would soon learn how it affected his own stay!
In those beauteous islands of his dreams of far away.

The scents of the flowers now made him to choke!
His throat would swell shut whenever he moaned or spoke,
Causing him struggle to get out ever a quiet croak!
At night, he tossed and turned and often times awoke.

Night and day, besieged lungs were bound and held so tight,
By the fruits of those pollens that never took flight!
He feared that he'd choke and die lonely in the night.
Every moment was struggle, every breath a good fight!

Dallion's eyes were running like the falls of that land.
His nose clogged or running, he could now barely stand!
Not even the healers were quite able to understand.
He'd stare for a ship, as he lay wasting in the sand.

Finally a mast appeared from the distant blue!
A white patch of hope he spied sailing through!
Then good news, it was docking for a whole day or maybe two!
He soon hugged his dear hosts and bid them all ado!

When the captain spied him grown so sickly and so thin,
He stated so directly, "Maybe we should throw him right back in!"
To save himself from disrespect, Dallion mustered up a grin,
Luckily the captain's heart of iron was wrought of softer tin!

Back aboard, the lad's old strength like the eagle's soon renewed!
It mattered not how rocked the deck or how the tempest spewed!
For his face was set for home. What marvels he had viewed!
Returning with the wonders of his dream pursued!

That Dallion Stall, all agreed, was never quite the same,
As the young man who'd left his home bearing that very name,
For even in the day to day, bright colors overcame,
As highly defective sinuses could never his brave spirit lame!

He was now a seasoned traveler who could draw from the writer's well!
For the folks back home, quite unannounced, he'd weave a minstrel's spell,
Of wondrous Isles of sandy shores where the salt waves swell!
How often he amazed them, one could never tell!

So although he was back home in the family shop,
In that ordinary town, where he'd pause and lean on his mop,
Washed by those waves of wonder that would never quite stop,
As he shared it with others, leaning on that plain prop.

Klindorn and Glengarth

There is a land that's washed by the oceans foamed wave.
Where the ships glide by as the seabirds rave,
And waters roar, then hiss like scared snakes
As over the sands glistening, it slowly now rakes.

But in this land so bounteous blessed by the sea
Is the common curse of a coastal country.
The pirates whose greed and lust for cold blood
Is a greater terror than the angry sea's flood.

The cruelty of man can outdo nature's wild wrath,
That wrath that destroys all good in its path,
But so to the noble that men have in their hearts
Can restore and mend things broken in parts.

Such a man was Haulcliff, King of Lazorn,
Who fell smitten in battle on one bloody morn.
But he beckoned to Klindorn his true trusted friend,
Before the bite of the steel had accomplished its end.

"Klindorn, I leave my son to your care.
Teach him to be brave and to do what is fair
Tell him, please, Klindorn, I don't want to leave him alone
But I must join his mother, where she has now flown."

So died Haulcliff, great lord of Tar Hall,
Mourned by the rich, the poor, and the small
And Klindorn reigned as steward instead,
Till Glengarth reached the age he could wed.

Nobly and justly reigned the steward Klindorn
And reared young Glengarth just as he'd been sworn
With love and attention as with both his two sons
In the knightly arts, they became the first ones.

As each evening would pull the dark night shade down,
Klindorn would sit with the three boys all round.
He would tell them of tales and lessons of life.
And they would listen to him till chased to bed by his wife.

So the boys grew in age, valor, and in wit.
And Klindorn's mind, they would try hard to pit
With answerless questions and problems of yore.
As they grew older, they steadily advanced more and more.

Guilefad the oldest was the best at this sport.
But his brother Dyfafil was quick to retort
Though not a match for Glengarth in wit or in war,
A master-at-arms and an expert in lore.

The day finally came when Glengarth took command
Of the royal brigade, the first in the land.
Astride his white hullox, Grotstel, with tassels of red
A goodly number of cavalry soldiers he led.

Now the hullox is a magnificent beast,
Like a snow white deer with four pronks at the least.
Where, on those antlers, the reins are held fastened tight.
A sturdy, true animal when engaged in a fight.

It soon became apparent; Glengarth was ready to reign.
His fame spread rapidly along the coast's plain.
Tall he sat between the antlers of white,
A man kind in peace but fierce in a fight.

*****

Into the house of Klindorn was born a grandson,
The first time he saw him, Klindorn's heart had been won.
He looked proudly on Guilefad and Larta, his wife.
The parents who'd brought about this new life.

How proud would Guilefad sit on the throne,
And his grandson could be a king respected and known.
But Klindorn was but steward, and Glengarth was heir.
The thought of this tragedy made a deep-anger flare.

How could Glengarth be driven away?
A permanent way, once gone, he must stay.
He'd kept more than his promise, and Haulcliff was dead.
Over and over in his feverish mind, he now said.

Through the tall castle gate, a currier rode.
From the eastern direction where the wide river flowed.
Dismounting his hullox to the steward's chamber he sped.
He was panting profusely; his face was all red.

"Lord, please forgive me for my wild, harried state!
It was necessary to hurry before it's too late.
The pirates, they've landed on the beach at Dunkay.
Their numbers are three hundred at least I would say!"

"Take care of this man," the steward gave word.
"Throw him in the dungeon, his story's absurd!
I'd received fair warning there would be such a trick
There are but fifty pirates! Now away with him quick!"

So the innocent man was thrown fast in chains,
Wondering why such a punishment and racking his brains!
But a plot had been spawned in the old steward's mind,
Like the sure spin of a spider, it was certain and well lined.

"Send for Glengarth," was the steward's command.
His luck had been better than he could have planned.
"Glengarth, take fifty strong men for the ride to Dunkay.
Pirates have landed make speed, you mustn't delay!"

*****

Out he ran quickly to muster his men.
So on the pirates, they could fiercely descend.
To stop the fiends before the pillaging was done,
Before the fields were wasted and they'd killed everyone!

He hoisted high the flag of Lazorn.
The seabirds flying and the great golden horn.
So waved the colors on the young prince's steed
As the troops pulled out with him in the lead,

Clad in shinning helmets and fine bluish mail.
They turned to the coast where the ships often sail,
Over the grasses that the wind does sway,
Through the mountain passes toward where the sea does lay.

On rode Glengarth, his brown eyes set fast.
No peace would he find till the battle had passed.
His light-brown hair would float in the wind.
To these bloodthirsty villains, he'd lost father and friend.

In a matter of hours, they drew near the coast.
Each man of them dreaming of the great victory toast
Over the last ridge and around the last bend,
Waiting for an enemy body to rend.

But it was they who were trapped by a superior force.
Like a beetle on an ant hill, there was no recourse.
The enemy hoard gave cries of delight
As they rushed wildly forward for a piece of the fight.

The scum and the dregs of each nation were there,
Where they'd vomited out from their island lair.
Tall Fargornorth traitors with fair skin and light hair,
Even Bimaroke vermin could be seen here and there.

Statuesque Klulu Chee with black skin and dark hearts,
Their almond eyes flashing as they raced forth like darts.
Vladyos villains of all statures and hues,
Depending on the nation from which each did ooze.

The mighty young prince was troubled quite sore.
Everywhere he looked came more and yet more.
All sordid and dirty, eager blades they did wave,
And Glengarth knew not one good man he could save.

"Fight boldly and make them pay dear.
Know well, for each man whose corpse you leave here,
Will be one less able to spread his foul fear,"
Saying this firmly a pirate head he did sear.

*****

The banner of Glengarth, he could still see,
When Klindorn turned to greet company,
It was Dyfafil, the younger and handsomer son,
Who'd come to visit his father, not knowing the work he had done.

"I heard the horn blast and the riders set out.
Tell me now what is my royal brother about?"
That phrase "royal brother" pierced Klindorn like steel,
And a lost dizzy sense, he began then to feel.

Though bantered in jest the phrase was meant true.
A great bond of spirit united those two,
And Guilefad, the elder, loved Prince Glengarth no less.
This crime to his sons he could never confess.

For each of the three he had molded by hand,
To love, honor, and courage and true justice demand.
They would never forgive Klindorn for this act of deceit,
Both would turn from their father and spit at his feet.

From his sons, this crime would be easy to hide,
But he could never silence that whisper, lisping inside.
He remembered back to those familiar fables of yore,
The one of Yagfarfil, he had told years before.

*****

When Sardil II felt the blade's curse,
Fears for his son troubled him first.
So upon Yagfarfil, he called in his need
And gave him command to obey what he heed.

To raise up young Smaglad to rule all Lazorn
With love for all justice and treachery, scorn.
So Smaglad was reared by the steward Yagfarfil.
Who followed in all things his late liege's will.

But Yagfarfil had children of his own in the house.
And as Smaglad grew older he often did grouse;
For his son, Smundane, would make a fine king,
So the evil Yagfarfil must see to the thing.

To be grandsire of kings was his burning desire!
It burnt in his mind as a ravenous fire.
He wouldn't be robbed; his mad dream he'd defend.
Smaglad must die before his day to ascend.

So to his chamber, he called his corrupted physician,
Who sunned in the court in his august position.
Saying, "Smaglad, you know has no great love for you sir,
You'll be out in the streets unless the right things do occur."

The doctor's old mouth twisted to smile.
"You know I've been troubled about that for a while,"
Speaking these words, he produced a small vile.
"The poison is here, all remains is our gile."

"You will toast to his health at the great feast tonight,
And the young fool will die before the first light."
So spoke the doctor with evil delight,
Filled with the poison of greed and cold spite.

Not known to the two there stood at the door,
The old nurse, Cladd, who was troubled quite sore,
For Smaglad had grown from a babe in her care.
She must see that the young prince escaped from the snare.

She watched the doctor closely as he poured in the brew,
Not worried at all, for she knew what to do.
Diverting all attention, she set about her task
Of saving her liege lord from a traitor's bright mask.

She poured the wine for the prince in a new cup,
Then cleaned his cup carefully before they did sup.
The steward's wine she poured there, so sparkling and inviting red
And the poisonous wine into the steward's cup fled.

The music of minstrels wafted joyously there in Tar Hall;
The guests were quite happy to accept such a call.
Seated at table was Yagfarfil, steward and lord,
His daughter, Yagmora, and Smundane "Brave Sword."

Young Smaglad, the prince, looked out over the guests
From his place at the head, he could see all the rest.
His bright eyes flashed happy at future subjects all round,
And he wished them good fortune and help of the crown.

The steward arose, his black hair shining bright.
And the gray in his beard made a soft silver light.
The cup of his doom held in his right hand,
He beckoned all in the hall now to stand.

"To Smaglad, the heir of the lands of Lazorn,
To Smaglad, the son of our land's highest born,
May he live to rule wisely and protect our fair coast,
To Smaglad, our prince, I drink now this toast!"

Giving a cheer, they all drank the red wine,
Refiling their cups, they prepared then to dine,
But soon the smile of Yagfarfil was destined to melt
As the effects of the venom were increasingly felt.

When most of the guests had taken their leave,
The treacherous steward began to totter and weave.
He held his wide stomach; he began then to shake,
His parlor went livid, a step he did take.

Pulling forth his great blade with a weakening grip,
He staggered back weakly and quite nearly did trip.
"Old doctor, you've betrayed me through stupidity or greed,"
And the steward ran him through before he could plead.

The tottering steward had strength for no more.
Giving a last moan, he flopped to the floor.
And so the two died trapped by their crime,
Immortalized as villains until the Lord ends this time.

Yes, death robbed Yagfarfil of the news he had sought,
For in his treacherous webs, it had alluded his thought.
That love between Smaglad and Yagmora had grown,
And true heirs of the throne would be of his own.

*****

And Klindorn remembered the three boys at his feet,
How their eyes would grow big as the tale he'd repeat.
They'd scoff at the steward who'd caused his own fall,
And joke of the fact they were descendants one and all.

For Klindorn and Haulcliff were first cousins in kin,
Both of them royal and proudhearted men,
Descendants of Yagmora and noble Smaglad,
As were many kings and heroes who lay beneath the cold sod.

But it was not the thought of the children that turned him inside,
A crime of such treason, he could never abide.
He jerked from the window and called his son,
In hopes that from treason, a victory could come.

Dispatch all the men, make them ready to ride.
Gather the troops up in Kleckthorn to help turn the tide.
Make steadily swift for the shores of Dunkay.
Take no time to daddle or rest on the way!

"Call to your brother, to take charge of Tar Hall!"
Shouting this loudly, he tore his shield from the wall.
"The blood of Yagfarfil flows thick in my veins,
I will personally lead our army on the proud plains."

These words fell strangely on Dyfafil's young ear.
His father should rest after battling many a year.
But never in his life had Klindorn been more upset,
And a delay of such action, Dyfafil thought he'd regret.

So he raced out of the room to do what his father had said.
Through corridors and chambers making ready he sped.
When all was made ready, Klindorn mounted his steed,
Making for the coast with all possible speed.

His bones had grown weary; his muscles were sore.
But he rode like a hero as he had long before.
It was with a great pain the steward crossed over the hills,
For he had greater concerns than mere physical ills.

Then in the distance, the battle horn blew,
And Klindorn rushed forward; he must hurry, he knew!
For each whistle of arrow or clacking of sword
Might be the echoing of the death of his young lord!

*****

The troops of Glengarth had barely started the fight
When their eyes were greeted by the so welcome sight!
For they had been lost victims of storm in the night,
With no hope of seeing the sweet morning light.

The eyes of Klindorn were ablaze in such wrath;
He hacked down the pirates who stood in his path.
And the troops of Lazorn poured down on the enemy host,
Like a thundering tidal wave crashing down on the coast.

Like spray of waves, the blood spouted out!
Crimson rivers of red gushed here and about.
The look of horror shone now in the foe
As through ranks of their numbers the army did mow.

And Klindorn the Brave led the attack.
When a Fargornorth ax smote him square in the back,
His men helped him to safety as best they could do.
Sword blades were flashing and arrows there flew.

Klulu Chee long spears stabbed through many a throat
But not nearly as many as the army did smote.
A blade was lodged in one Fargornorth scum;
It crashed through his shoulder but loose would not come.

As the soldier struggled to free his trapped blade,
A rally of fierce enemy arrows then sprayed,
One finding it's mark in the young trooper's ear,
His face twisted horribly in pain and great fear!

A Bimaroke vermin who stood there in the way
Was run through by the antlers of a hullox that day.
The poor animal staggered with his victim's foul weight,
But a trooper dislodged him before it was too late.

A Vladyo bandit was heard to give a shrill cry,
As from his right arm, his right hand did fly high.
But of little consequence it was since soon he did die,
And joined the disfigured forms that on the ground there did lie.

The hullox of the sergeant was knocked to the ground,
And he was cast on the growing death mound.
As he dropped, he landed on an upturned spear,
And he heard a faint laugh as the cruel blade did sear.

The sword of Glengarth found a Klulu Chee's head.
It flashed silver downward and ascended quite red.
One half of the head flopped flat on one side.
The other half followed the neck on the ride.

The mounds of the fallen were growing quite tall.
The hullox began tripping, and many did fall.
Some of the helpless who were wounded quite sore
Were crushed by the hullox and then lived no more.

Glengarth and others were then forced to dismount,
But astride or afoot, they gave true account.
The antlers of some hullox were turning quite red,
As they gorged a foul pirate until he was dead.

Slowly but surely the pirates lost ground
When the air was broken by another shrill sound.
It was the horn of Dyfafil and the troops of Kleckthorn
Who charged at the pirates who were already forlorn.

Ships from Kleckthorn emerged on the vile fleet
To bring to completion the pirate's defeat!
Evening was dawning, but the pirates fought on.
A pirate fights fiercely when put hard upon.

Antlers of hullox and swords of Lazorn
Ram through the bodies already blade torn.
Now and again was heard the loud crack of a Bimaroke head,
As quicker and quicker, the pirates flopped dead.

Some of the pirates made it back to their fleet.
But the ships of Kleckthorn would pursue this defeat.
Small boats were lowered from two pirate bark
As they strove for the flagship to unite before dark.

They had hardly arrived before the flagship caught fire.
As the arrows of the defenders made the flames grow higher.
The fires on the sails could be seen on the sea
As the sun took its light from where they could see.

The ship and its image could both now be seen.
The flames from the vessel gave the waters a sheen.
As pieces of rigging fell from the main mast,
Other pieces fell up from the reflection it cast.

The fire on the deck made the boards start to pop
As those who were able into the sea tried to drop.
But none of them made it; every pirate was slain,
Except one jabbering Vladyo who was completely insane.

Many men had been wasted; the battle was done.
The greatest victory over pirates since that day was won!
The shores of Lazorn were calmed for some time,
Before a single pirate in that land again committed a crime.

The battle was over; the damage was done.
Though for many on the beach, the war had begun
To live a life wholly when pieces are gone,
Missing an arm or a limb, they were doomed to live on.

They are fools who sing of the battle's great glory.
A fight to the death is only bloody and gory.
A horrible answer to that selfish, closed mind
That can think only to ravage at the expense of mankind.

The pirates understood nothing less than the blade.
It was their type of decision that had to be made.
How no more would they ravage the Moordarey lands.

Yet before the pirates sail did burn bright,
Illuminating that glorious, terrible sight,
Glengarth found where Klindorn lay sore.
The old steward signaled, he had to settle the score.

"Klindorn, great steward, you should have stayed back
And let another lead the major attack!
Why couldn't you rest far from harm's way?
You have saddened my heart on this great victory day.

"I will call Dyfafil and take his place in the fight,
That he may once more be revealed to your sight."
"No, Glengarth, there is no time to draw him now back.
See how strong my young boy leads the attack?

"I betrayed you, my stepson, as Yagfarfil of old.
I am here not because I'm gallant and bold.
It was because the price for my crime must be paid.
That I, Klindorn the Traitor, led that last raid!

"All Lazorn must know why I died here,
They mustn't make me a hero like those we revere.
No, Klindorn the Sinner is who you have found
Lying here justly, like a lump on the ground."

Glengarth the Bold burst into sad tears
As he hugged the man who was a father for years.
And Klindorn the Steward knew his love was not lost.
He thanked the great Lord despite the high cost.

"The name of Klindorn will have great honor in Tar Hall.
I will hide nought from our people, they will know all,
And hail Klindorn as hero and a man of great heart!
Minstrels will apply your deeds to their arts."

So Klindorn the Steward died honored that way.
And in the halls of Lazorn, he is still honored today.
But more important than mere hero's laud,
He died at peace with himself and with God.

Section 2
Earth

The Storyteller

The morning sun rises slowly over the village shops,
And at the door of such a place, a bundled figure stops
And asks himself if this may be a bright and better day,
If he might taste accomplishment along the tedious way.

He passes by his comrades at work at their benches there,
To find his place inconspicuous, shaded by the stair,
And he faces the task before him with a hopeless glare,
Not daring to achieve precision work of a craftsman care.

For him, there are no great successes that give his heart a swell,
Just the hollow clack of a lonely bucket echoing from an empty well.
His striving for an excellence to give pride to a working day,
Somehow seems defeated by those calls of far away!

Those calls crash through the boxes that hold the order of the day,
That necessary order that leashes the mind to stay.
And concentrate its vast power to a fine precision line.
To produce a worthy work that satisfies like wine.

Ah, but alas, for our poor worker has not the craftsman mind.
Instead it bolts like a stallion, pursuing wonders of every kind,
To set free kings in kingdoms and reveal the hero lad,
To call men to quests of daring and cheer children when they are sad.

Within his ken, there is a world at least as vast as earth,
Filled with men and magic, marvels and with mirth.
That they cry within his spirit for the labor of their birth,
But he fears to consider even the greatest of them of an actual worth.

He says, "Ah, to be a minstrel, a singer, and a bard,
To rove the green fair countryside in route to a gay courtyard!
To enchant the lords and the peasant lads while filling up my glass,
And catching the magic glowing forth in the eyes of a comely lass!

But I can't wonder forth and leave my dear ones wanting,
For the love I have for them would ere be the more haunting
Since God created man to share and be succor to his kin.
Not to be seduced foolishly, down the paths of sin!

So as dragging by the hours and dragging by the years,
His life is held prisoner by all of those dreadful fears,
That some might not will to ride beside his mighty kings,
Or love his gentle peasant folk with their simple things.

It troubled his heart to picture his heroes turned aside
Or those lands distained in which he took such pride.
He thought, *Who cares but I and a chosen few*
What in my world any of these may say or do!

Then he stared out wistfully from the window where the light came in
And turned his attention back to work so he might begin.
So each day took its toll on his imprisoned soul,
Making him seem less the man and more and more the mole.

He heard the priest when Sunday came, preach on use of talent,
About how the man who invested well received the reward of the
    gallant,
And he prayed, "Dear Lord, set me free to use what I was given."
"My son," God said, "try and believe, and all will be forgiven."

When Mass was done, he turned away and stepped out into the light,
Spying there his friend the scribe who, in his tales, took such delight.
"My friend, I must talk with you of things deep on my heart."
Laughed the scribe. "With good food and wine, we'll have a better start!"

Then relished the pair their simple fair as the elder made request:
To find himself and show the world that which he could do best.
Where upon answered the scribe, "I don't really know, but this I will
    suggest,
I will make script of all you say and leave to the Lord the rest."

For hours, many an evening these two now steadily met
And toiled and argued through the night long after the sun had set,
At times, they felt like brothers, and at others, they cursed, they met,
Until each line was set in place by love and tears and sweat.

When the partners realized that their task was cleverly done,
They laughed, talked, and drank a toast to the rising of the sun.
But then dragged to work that morning two exhausted men
Whose joyous spirits wakened them till they could leave again.

But neither could anticipate the wait which followed next,
Sweeping the two into arguments as they grew now more perplexed.
Then the frustrating labor bore worse fruit at our worker's shop
Till he would lash out at his family though he strived to stop.

Now fear of failure began to eat upon his faltering nerve,
"Why, my God, does this happen to me? It's more than I deserve."
Still his employer's face was setting ever serious and grim.
And at home, his wife and children were wondering what's so wrong
    with him.

Now providing for his family became the burning concern
Of the struggling story wright who battled now to earn!
Not until he handed it back to God where it all belonged
Was he able to recover that peace and correct where he had wronged.

So on, much as in the beginning, the storyteller dwelt,
Working on and earning bread until the snows did melt,
When upon his pondering thoughts did so suddenly spring
A voice so loud and full of joy, it made his whole shop ring!

For there stood tall the comely scribe with his eyes a twinkle,
So his cohort started right up with his brow a wrinkle,
"Ha, you fool sit at your bench without even rising!
As I am the bearer of good news as you must be surmising!"

"The committee of the festival are enchanted by our tales,
Come, my friend, tomorrow, and they'll give us the details.
They said with plays as fit as these our fame will all abound
As gents and ladies travel here to hear from all around!"

Up jumped the weary storyteller with such dancing feet,
That the odd pair continued this, prancing into the street!
The village people stopped and stared deciding they were drunk,
Not realizing they were captains whose cargo had not sunk!

And so the players performed his work upon the wooden stage,
Making the characters come to life from the scribe's fine page.
So now his kings had rightfully come into their reign,
While his simple heroes battled brave across the blood-soaked plain.

The storyteller noticed his characters reborn into the crowd!
And his once bound, bridled spirit soared now strong and proud.
But upon his lips came forth a humble plea,
"Oh, Lord, above release those yet bound like you just did me!"

Birdland Bedlamb

The precinct house in Birdland was in an awful mess.
You'd think it was run by birdbrains or those who knew much less.
The chief of the proud station was going raven mad,
For the place was filled with cuckoos making things quite bad.

Just that very morning some thugs had flown the coop.
Except for one fat chicken who was afraid to join the troop.
So half the force was out to seize the robin's roost.
While the troops best officer was flying high, quite juiced.

A defiant old jaywalker was grousing in protest,
Claiming unjust injury, concerning her arrest,
While a mischief making mockingbird was mimicking her mournful sound,
And a fat old goosey gander lay marinated on the ground.

A sharp night owl was staring, checking out the foxy chicks,
His legal eagle trying all his legal tricks.
The drunken goose kept honking all this dreadful time,
"Can anyone of you fine fowl please sparrow me a dime?"

Joining in the clucking mess, protesters were brought in.
It seemed the doves and hawks were now joining in the din.
And his eminence the cardinal was immediately under fire
Since one of the doves arrested was the forest friar.

A dodo bird came crashing through the station door
And proceeded quite naturally to fall upon the floor.
By the desk, a mother hen clucked about her wayward son.
Though he was a homing pigeon, he was a roving one.

The lovebirds were squawking in an angry fit,
Refusing to koo for the sergeant just a little bit.
Just then the officers entered with the getaway flock,
And the popinjay in the corner had someone else to mock.

As soon as they were questioned, one began to sing,
Telling his inquisitors willingly every little thing.
"Shut up, you lousy stool pigeon!" yelled a comrade of the crime.
"You're a yellow-bellied sapsucker, I knew it all the time!"

The jailbirds were escorted safely to the back.
Then an irate duck came waddling in with an angry quack.
The nightingale across the marsh was keeping him awake,
So the music-loving hummingbird told him to jump into the lake.

A military bird walked up in search of an AWOL stork,
And some of the doves were shouting away with that dumb dork!
At last, the drunken goose had conned himself a dime,
From the hapless dodo bird who couldn't guess his rhyme.

The poor old chief then starred up with a squawk of disbelief,
For into that wretched door had come his new relief.
He greeted this good pigeon with hale and happy words,
"I'm going home, goodbye, good luck! This place is for the birds."

Sea Drudge

When I trod the road to Trent,
I met on the way a man named Gent,
And sailed, we two the frothy sea,
Where stormed the waves with dampened glee.

And from the mast appeared to me on a tempestuous spew,
Through mist of tide and endless space forms that once I knew,
Above the waves of salt and such, a fish of winged blue.
Thoughts of chill and chicken pox did that fish pursue.

Yes, in the armpits of my mind, there flew the winged fish,
And tartar sauce and lemon peel to garnish such a dish.

The Droggy Brother

T'was late that night, I finished my cup
When I, from my easy chair, rose up,
To wake my brother from his sleep,
But he was engaged in slumber deep.

I shook his arm as you well might
If you wished to rouse one late at night.
And I then perceived his open eyes
That cleverly concealed that sleep's disguise.

He arose from the couch and turned down the hall,
And it clearly seemed that, that was all.
But passing his bedroom, he continued some more
Until he had opened, in error, the closet door.

He stood there and stared till I called out his name.
Then he went to the next door and did just the same.
But this was the place where the heating unit was kept
And not at all like the place where he slept.

I touched him again, and again, he did stray
Into the bathroom the usual way,
And I thought, *All is over, now to my bed.*
But alas, poor Patrick had need to be led.

Elephant Titus

There once was an elephant, Titus,
Who threw a party which failed to excite us.
He got so darn drunk,
He tripped over his trunk!
Which served him right since he didn't invite us.

Bored to Tears

Bored to tears, yes, bored to tears!
Barney the Builder was bored to tears.
He carried boards up to tiers.
He carried and carried for a dozen years!

No matter how many boards went up those tiers,
More were needed as completion nears.
Then new tiers were needed to maintain careers,
So Barney the Builder was bored to tears!

Frank N. Sense and His Fantastic Sidewalk Sail

Gather my children, come and hear!
Look to the sky, and it may appear.
What's in the heavens? How does it steer?
Hush, ye children, and I'll make it all clear!

Little Frank N. Sense was poor as dirt.
His dad always wore a torn T-shirt.
His illiterate mother was sharp and curt.
His ragged sister had just one skirt!

Life, it seemed, would stay quite bad
With an abusive mother and a drunkard dad.
He wanted to believe, but he felt so sad
When he looked around to see all he had.

One day, his daddy called him to his knee
And said to his son, "This is how it will be.
You have to live with your grandma, Bea,
Who lives on the corner of Main and C."

Well, Grandma's house was a sorry shack
With a cute little outhouse placed out back.
The whole place would shake when the train crossed the track.
But at Grandma's table, there was never a lack!

Grandma, who was poor, banked a richness within,
And Frank became grateful that they were both kin.
He wasn't now hungry; he wasn't so thin.
The new possibilities made his head spin.

For twelve more years, he learned, and he grew.
Grandma was keeping secrets; this he well knew.
Things unexplainable would sometimes ensue.
The mysteries that abounded were more than a few!

A day of sadness fell like the night.
He came home from college feeling all right,
But his eyes then fell on a terrible sight!
Gone from her face was the glow of life's light!

Days of sadness, nights of woe!
A pain that clutches and can't let go,
Reflected in those images as he went to and fro,
In familiar surroundings, she had taught him to know.

Would the reading of the will his family unite?
T'would be tomorrow, he was sad and uptight.
He tossed, and he turned all through that dark night,
But he rose with a sense that it might be all right.

Frank went to the lawyer, but he sat all alone.
Seems he was the only one to have shown,
For Grandma was poor, as it is well known
And undervalued by the seed she had sown.

The lawyer looked sad; he'd been Grandma's old friend.
He tried to smile as his hand did extend,
But it hurt that the old woman had had such an end,
That only one grandchild had found time to spend.

"Well, Frank," he said, "it all goes to you.
It's not surprising that she found it your due,
Considering all of the things you've been through.
It all ended up being just you two."

But now there were not two but only just one.
Without his grandma, was he still a grandson?
What could he say? What could be done?
Emptiness gripped him; there was no place to run!

"Here's an interesting note," the lawyer broke in.
Bringing Frank back as his head took a spin.
He stared at the barrister so gaunt and so slim,
Trying to deal with the loss of his kin.

"She states that piece of sidewalk, that's no more than a shard,
That runs north and south in front of her yard
Belongs solely to you, not City Oxnard.
She wrote its description right down on this card."

Taking the card, it said a bit more,
Stating Grandma's own father had completed that chore.
But why such a fragment of nine feet and no more?
"There's a note in the cookie jar with the rest of the lore."

Curiosity had temporarily relieved the sheer grief.
It had all turned so strange; it challenged belief!
Frank's farewell to the lawyer was awkward and brief.
He dashed home to the cookie jar to find some relief.

He pulled the old cookie jar down from the stand
And searched the bottom as Grandma had planned,
Till he found an envelope the color of sand,
To find the strange words in Grandma's own hand.

"My father was a sailing man before the birth of this century.
He voyaged to far off places to see what could possibly be,
And in the secret places of the world, he came upon great mystery,
Hidden in the islands of the southern sea.

"On a small island where they stopped to trade,
The storms came early, so there they stayed.
And a chief's life he saved, while so delayed,
Who became a truer friend than he ever had made.

"The prospect of leaving made heavy his heart,
And the chief had laid plans before he'd depart,
Taking him to a cave in the most secret part,
And that's where this legend had its true start!

"'We two together must perform a small task,'
Stated the chief before my daddy could ask.
From under a rock, he pulled a small cask.
His excitement and mystery were impossible to mask!

"Deep in the night when the stars twinkled high,
I saw our destinies inscribed in the sky,
And I fell into a dream that came by and by.
Listen and I'll tell you, so you'll stop asking why.

"Soon you must leave, but our friendship will last,
Far in the future to return from the past.
Help me fashion a sail equipped with a mast,
And I swear our friendship will bind us quite fast.

"Starting that evening, they worked on for days,
Convincing my father, t'was more than a phase.
The chief labored on as if caught up in a daze,
Then he told my old pappy things to amaze!

"After you leave, we'll no longer here meet,
Till your great Christian God calls us home to His seat.
We'll savor this time as something so sweet,
Together as we accomplish this nautical feat.

"Our friendship will live forever in those of our line,
Your descendant's return will be wonderfully fine,
For he'll save a life of my own as you have done mine,
And the two of them like one rope intertwine.

"From their own bloodlines will eventually flow,
A family from us, yes, this I know.
Our friendship is the seed to make this thing grow,
A sturdy tree that will take root rather slow."

"When they finished the sail, the chief gave him some sand,
'This is to make sure he returns to this land.
Fashion something sturdy to make the mast stand.
Your seed will return just how it was planned.'

"My father returned and built a house on this lot.
He hid the mast and sail where they'd never know rot,
For the words of his friend, he'd never forgot,
And he poured the sand in the sidewalk on this very spot.

"My children were not worthy to my greatest pain.
They had no imagination, just selfish disdain.
What could I tell them? How'd I explain?
But you came into my life, and you know I am sane.

"Know I watch you always from heaven above.
You'll never be a day apart from my love.
And you'll fly through the clouds on wings of a dove,
If you take fear and faintness and give it a shove!"

So he found the place the sail had been hid,
Where none less visionary would seek to get rid.
He heard the creak as he stretched back that old lid,
To find it under hides made out of black kid.

A colorful sail of reds, blues, and greens,
Reminiscent of tropical south island scenes,
Birthed images of beaches and svelte island queens,
Relayed to his mind's eye by colorful skeins.

When the sky was well black, the streetlight shone dim,
He looked at the job now waiting for him.
Frank felt kind of stupid, so he sang and old hymn.
The chance of this working seemed ridiculously slim.

Even in the darkness, he spied odd patches of stone,
Which he could remove with hand tools alone.
They had covered the mast holes as the pale moonlight shone.
As he fitted mast fast to sidewalk, he faced the unknown.

What did he expect there on dry city ground?
There wasn't a body of water for miles to be found.
But yet to his ears came a low far-off sound,
What happened at that moment could only astound!

The whole masted sidewalk rose straight up from the soil
With amazed Frank aboard in a state of turmoil!
Higher above our own earthly coil
Till no building or sign could his view spoil.

With the guide ropes, he turned straight into the west,
Practicing riding the winds when they blew at their crest.
He concentrated carefully, always trying his best
Till he could safely sail right by a bird's hidden nest.

How to get down? He feared a great fall!
To splat on the ground didn't seem good at all!
He tried to lower the sail, but fear made him stall.
Would his sidewalk pitch like a floundering yawl?

His hands were now trembling; his throat felt all dry.
A sidewalk surely wasn't a thing one should fly!
Frank had to have courage; he knew he must try.
He lowered the sail to descend by and by.

Back on the ground, he must struggle for nerve.
He couldn't allow now for his courage to swerve.
He needed to return back to that curve,
By his grandmother's house, its hanger to serve.

Frank took a deep breath, and it took him a while,
But he soon lifted off with a professional style,
Rising quite smoothly over the roofs made of tile,
Till he landed at Grandma's and leapt off with a smile.

"I must disassemble the sail, else the neighbors will see,
This very strange sight that just couldn't be.
Oh! The questions they'd ask are all bewildering to me.
I've been lucky so far, it's true!" then said he.

As time passed away, he became skillful and bolder
And tired had he grown of looking over his shoulder.
The travel lust in him, like a fire, now did smolder.
"I need to be off 'fore I grow any older."

Now so encouraged, he longed to be free!
To know different zones in his native country,
He remained on overland routes, for he feared the great sea,
But he became just so happy, yes, just happy to be!

People all over in small towns and farms
Would point to the heavens and wave with their arms,
Where he would then land and partake of their charms.
They'd feed him and lodge him with no further alarms.

Small papers would do stories, he'd collect a few fees
And travel all over or rest at his ease,
Doing just about whatever he please,
Thanking the good Lord each day on his knees.

As winter was nearing, his thoughts turned to home.
When weather got warmer, he continued to roam
Back to Oxnard and Ventura where the sand meets the foam.
His sidewalk could rest in its own native loam.

So he transversed places of interest all over his map,
Over acres of wheat and the Grand Canyon's great gap,
Up the Rocky's great peaks, all laid out at his lap.
He navigated them easily; it was all such a snap!

As he crossed California's great desert, he became sort of sad.
He'd lost everyone whom he ever had had.
An institution had Mom, and drinking drowned his dad,
His sister had married to forget all that was bad.

Aunts and uncles had disappeared over the years,
Despising their origins with insults and with jeers,
Even forsaking their mother despite her true tears.
With that, all sense of belonging just disappears.

The wondrous sidewalk had interrupted his grief,
Which originally was both quiet and brief,
Now all of his sorrows hit him in gigantic relief.
The emptiness and loneliness were beyond all belief!

So his tears fell like puddles on stone.
It echoed to him, "Frank, you're alone, you're alone!"
He didn't even notice he was drenched, wet to the bone.
His tears mixed with raindrops over the surface he'd flown.

The wind became violent as he neared his home coast;
His fists clenched tightly to the sail's wooden post.
It had always been easy; he'd heard himself boast.
Now he was involved in a struggle that would have petrified most!

Frank tied himself on; it was impossible to steer,
Not till this storm had started to clear.
He was now cradled in the cold arms of fear
Whose dubious comfort had dried every tear.

The battering winds blew him straight out to sea.
Frank now had no idea where in the world he could be!
Things didn't calm till the dawn of day three.
It seemed he'd been blasted and blown eternally.

He'd fought to hold tight; he'd thought he'd soon die
And drop like a pelican into the sea from the sky.
All of his efforts were drained from continuing to fly.
When the skies finally calmed, he started to cry.

Blessed sleep now claimed huge clouds of his time
As his unusual vessel continued to climb.
He missed that view of sunset's sublime
Till he woke to drink a flat lemon lime.

His ice chest had been stocked by generous fans,
Who had welcomed him warmly as he passed by their lands.
Now there remained a few bottles and cans,
A little lunch meat and snacks from some stands.

When he woke and rested, he felt free from the fear.
Since he knew not where he was, he couldn't be clear.
Would his decisions take him far or bring him quite near?
Without knowing the answer, he tried not to steer.

Exhaustion gripped him so tightly; he was then in and then out.
He had no idea how long he'd been blown thereabout.
As hard as he tried, he couldn't imagine his route
Frank just thanked God for his life, why should he pout?

Frank's food and drink were now nearly gone.
Without a place to land, he sailed on and on.
He was tired of the sidewalk and longed for a lawn.
He was weary, hungry, thirsty, and drawn.

Then all of a sudden, he woke with a jolt!
And grabbed the ropes like a fierce lightning bolt!
The sidewalk veered to the right and jumped like a colt.
This was no time to lag like some groggy-eyed dolt!

The cone of a volcano loomed straight ahead.
"Oh great, just another chance for me to get dead!"
The scream of a young woman now rang in his head,
And he stared down in safety from his high concrete bed.

A young woman was climbing at a furious gait,
Pursuing men behind her gave account for her state!
Up she toiled on that steep, sharp, jagged grate.
Death over capture, she'd accept for her fate.

Frank saw her slip, and she dropped like doomed stone!
He was close enough now to hear her sharp groan,
But she hit a small ledge, there standing alone,
Clinging there helpless below the mouth of a cone!

Frank's heart burst in pity as he captained his ship.
He must save her now quickly before she could slip!
His vessel responded at an incredible clip.
He reached for the maiden and felt her strong grip.

She came then onboard, too frightened to ask,
Her hands were all bloodied, her face a pale mask.
She then quickly fainted from her terror and task,
So Frank gently pressed to her lips a small silver flask.

Her eyes slowly opened so gentle and browned.
She was nothing short of lovely, slender, yet round,
The most beautiful creature he ever had found.
She looked up at his face and made a sharp sound.

She then looked in amazement at the craft where she lay,
Startled yet grateful. What could she say?
Frank kind of blushed at the awkward delay
Till her plea struck his ears. "We must get away!"

"Where? I don't know where I'm going or where I am at."
"I'd say you did a good job considering all that!"
So saying she pointed the way from where she now sat,
Toward a neighboring island, more sandy and flat.

"I have friends at the mission over that way,"
Spoke the perch plucked passenger after a proper delay.
"They'll hide us and feed us as long as we stay
And give me a chance to think and to pray.

"My father was Christian, so you can see
He baptized me for Mary Star of the Sea,
But the name, Star, is what they call me,
And that's who I've always been glad to be.

"My father died, and my uncle became chief.
He did not share our sacred belief.
Unlike my father, he's a liar and a thief.
He was trying to sell me to enlarge his small fief.

"I would rather meet death than marry that man,
Wicked and old, by my uncles own plan!"
Flushed suddenly with anger, she used her hand as a fan,
"So when I got the chance, I ran, and I ran!

"Do you speak English? I only presumed."
Frank nodded his head slowly, totally consumed.
For her hair was jet-black and seemed gently perfumed
Since Frank was struck silent she intently resumed.

"I've never seen such a thing. How can it fly?
When one minute, I'm perched on a ledge set to die,
Then like a winged hero, you fall from the sky!
I can't figure it out. Can you please tell me why?"

Frank made ready to answer, but Star was too quick,
"Tell me, could your last name be Thwick?"
He shook his head slowly. What an odd question to pick.
She said, "Just a legend I heard once when I was sick."

Frank's tongue came untied as her question hit base.
"I believe my great grandfather once came to this place.
He was Thadius Thwick who saved a chief of your race."
Frank saw his own answer in the lines of her face.

Star nodded her head, and he could tell that she knew.
"Then the legend of Great-Grandfather was actually true!
It wasn't about just someone but about me and about you!
You saved my life, in an instant, flying out of the blue!"

Frank nodded, amazed at what had occurred.
They each shared what they'd read now or possibly heard.
It couldn't be true. It was all so absurd!
But they sat, living proof of each legend word.

They stayed at the mission for less than a week from that day,
As they feared her uncle, if they dared there to stay,
But they rested up nicely and plotted their way
And left the blessed mission without further delay.

Before their departure, they got the priest to agree
To join them together till eternity.
So Francis Ned Sense took Mary Star of the Sea,
And they joined there together in blessed matrimony.

There was a kinship between them, hard to explain,
A holy combination like sunshine and rain.
They could feel the other's enjoyment and the other one's pain.
That they were meant for each other was obviously plain.

The priest booked passage on an outgoing ship,
For to sail on the sidewalk would be a hazardous trip,
And though our young Frank had Star fast in his grip,
He knew he would die if he allowed her to slip.

For the great adventure of riding the kite,
The captain granted passage with nary a fight.
For Frank would be captain in the dark of the night
When he and ship's captain would most often alight.

One dawn, before sunset near Wilmington's Port,
Star and Frank sailed the sky for the distance was short.
But they were spied here and there, so there came a report.
So after they landed, Frank delayed their retort.

It was finally settled just how it would be.
Frank sold to the "Enquirer" for quite a nice fee,
While Star's tale sold to the "Star" as it should naturally.
So with their nest egg, they now had the key.

Frank met a good partner named Kevin T Mur,
A true sailing man with a heart that was sure.
His wife, Katey, made Star's friendship a thing to endure,
So in business and friendship, everything was all pure.

They opened a factory where sails they now made,
Some with wondrous colors that the sun could not fade.
While none of them flew, all of them paid.
In the evenings, they visit and drink lemonade.

The wives opened a shop named after each mate.
The business in spices and imports was just great.
With the name, Frank N. Sense and Mur, it just had to rate.
They raised up nice families in this happy estate.

Over thirty-five years from that time now has passed,
Since timid young Frank found that old wooden mast,
More than thirty-five years since he first held Star, oh, so fast,
But there is still more to come, they're not at the last.

For late in the evening, when the stars twinkle their light,
He brings his own Star to sail off in the night.
With a hand full of grandkids who howl in delight,
They laugh, and they giggle as the sidewalk takes flight.

There in the air on their flying carpet of stone,
Grandpa and Grandma tell them those tails of their own.
Nothing can intrude on the magic as they soar all alone
As the grandparents will not tolerate a cellular phone.

"Grandma Star, tell us a story!" is the popular request.
"We always like the ones that you tell us best."
For Star outtalks Frank in both earnest and jest.
She fills her tales with wonder and marvelous zest!

Now Frank sits silent, blessed deep to the bone.
He now has a family; he's not all alone.
In the night's sky, he hugs the seeds he has sown,
From traveling the heavens where the winds have him blown.

On voyages like these, there comes a strange hush;
With his starlight on board, Frank is feeling no rush.
Star runs playful fingers through his hair, yet so thick and so lush.
The kids riding with them are all used to this mush.

The young talk to no one about their flights in the night.
What teacher or friend would believe a sidewalk in flight?
Will they have their own adventures on this great concrete kite?
Between you and me, I think they just might.

The Opera Tuna Tea

"Come and see. Get yourself free!
To attend the Opera Tuna Tea!
Classiest affair in the whole wide sea!
Join us all for there is no fee!"

So the ads floated everywhere,
To attend the grand gala and abandon care!
Fish and flounders by school or by pair,
All attended and paid no fare.

The tea was the best that sunk long ago,
In man-made ships, which inspired this show.
Operatic costumes and scores, you might know,
All were found there where the salt currents flow.

Vivaldi, Verde, and Wagner, all would be sung!
After currents had that old ship's bell rung,
Like a barnacle covered ghost from where it still hung.
While latecomers would crowd between and among.

However, the elegance of the tea must come first.
Each dainty serving minnow was well over rehearsed.
The tea would be sipped slowly with no clumsy burst,
Since at the bottom of the sea, there is so little thirst.

Splendid garibaldi with their armor of gold
Were recruited to aid this sophisticate fold.
Serving as waiters and ushers, twofold,
Looking quite smart, officious, and bold!

Since tunas are tunas, they carry such tune!
Their reputations carried quicker than soon!
Flying fish as their airmail proved a great boon.
Organizers had been working since early in June!

Finally, it came, the day of the tea!
To summon up swiftly the fish of the sea.
The performers bedecked in such finery,
Their friends soon forgot just who they might be!

"Oh my!" They all gasped. "Such posh and such style!"
Treats for the eye and the ear to beguile!
Attendees would stop just to stare for a while,
As into their proper seats they did file.

The tea was exquisite when the music did rise,
As a tuxedoed fat tuna caught all of their eyes.
His voice of a tenor evoked fair surprise,
Inspiring praise and long drawn out sighs!

So it continued as the fish now did swim,
On notes strong and sweet of the opera's sweet hymn,
Filling their hearts and mind to the brim,
Not noticing that they danced too close to the rim!

For all in a sudden, the tunas attacked,
Gobbling up the audience that they'd lured for a snack!
Frightened sea creatures tried to turn back,
To wide open mouths, where they only saw black!

All the tunas were bloated; one called for a beer!
A full happy bunch, they were full of good cheer!
As the finest of operas, the one without peer,
Was for its founders, the great fish feed of the year!

For the tuna has a longer memory than most,
Which annually enables him to play the great host,
To memorize choruses and propose a fine toast,
Making a spectacle of which they can boast!

In truth, most dull fishes have memory so short,
That in no time at all, they forget their report,
Which allow the tuna their annual sport,
As their victims never remember details of that sort!

Since the stupid audience never has even a hunch.
The hosts are happy to entertain the whole bunch
With fine tea and opera and a morsel to munch,
Until their alarmed guests provide them with lunch!

Creativity and work, wed there in the sea,
Exercised artfully like one family,
Opportunity birthed by tunas to be
Known as the great Opera Tuna Tea!

Desert Sands

The desert sands erased the trails,
Blown by winds that capture sails,
Gliding barges down the Nile,
Under the hungry eye of crocodile.

Such a hot unforgiving land,
Sun-filled days bake the sand,
Where ancient wonders defiant stand.
Eons gone by genius planned!

Pharaohs gone, and gods forgotten,
From this land, our origins begotten,
Why in a place so uninviting?
Our imaginations still exciting!

The Heir of Castle McCloor

Out from the village and across the murky moor,
Strolled the new heir to old Castle McCloor.
The lawyer, MacLockly, walked by his side
And spoke of the history of that land with great pride.

The father of the young heir had left years before.
He'd fought with his father and was thrown out the door.
So from the Scottish Highlands to America, he sailed,
Never to return to the land from whence he had hailed.

The father of our heir had married his wife late,
So there was none other to claim the estate.
Because he bore his sire's memory with bitterness and scorn,
His father refused to return to that place he was born.

The younger McCloor, after his father was dead,
Had far different thoughts dancing about in his head.
He was heir to a castle and the lands far away.
He'd collect his inheritance and possibly stay.

All his illusions of grandeur had now passed,
For the fog of that desolate moor hung on fast,
Causing unearthly forms to appear and then fade,
Through that lonely mist, they continued to wade.

All the while, MacLockly told of battles and blood,
Of clansmen's frames still found in the mud,
Where wounded, they struggled as they drowned in the slime
So that bones would emerge once buried in time.

So up the hill to the castle, the two of them strode,
For years of neglect had covered the old road.
At the portal, they paused to take in the main court,
Ancient cold towers of the medieval sort.

The fog and the dusk had concealed the top view.
It was difficult to tell what was imagined or true,
For each step ahead was like a step back,
As time building on had left there a crack.

It filled young McCloor with history's keen sense,
As MacLockly told tales of the castles defense.
He could nigh see his ancestors and the flash of cold steel
And hear the pipes blowing as the battle did reel.

Out of his pocket, MacLockly pulled the old key,
To open the door for the new heir to see,
The ancient halls of his own ancestry,
In this highland homeland across the sea.

Entering the castle, MacLockly told the heir all,
Of each piece of furniture, no object too small,
And of the ancient McCloors whose portraits lined the cold rooms,
How each lived till they met their own dooms.

The guest found his host, both keen and polite.
And in the stories of his guest, the host found delight.
The towers and the dungeon remained to be seen,
and the darkness had rendered the viewing time lean.

"Will you come back tomorrow?" he said, pouring the wine.
"You can come with your wife to the castle to dine.
And show me those high towers and the dungeon below."
But MacLockly shook his head as if to say no.

"I'll be glad te give ye a tour-r of th' tower-rs.
Ach, there's enough there te take several hour-rs.
But I'll no go doen te that tor-rtur-re lair.
Te many men have met their-r deaths doen there.

"Aye, I've heard stor-ries of th' rack en other-r tor-rtur-re devices,
Ir-ron maidens en chains en bone cr-rushing vices.
Wher-re men have begged to cr-ross deaths bloody door,
Only to endur-re and suffer-r ever-r th' mor-re."

"But surely such artifacts don't belong in a hole,
There in concealment, not being seen by a soul.
Surely you can't condone such a historic waste.
What can you possibly fear in that place?"

"Certain things belong in holes where they're buried,
And not from their'r unholy tombs to be carried.
Aye, many bizarre tales from this castle have grown,
En I'm wise enough te fear'r th' unknown!"

"Thank you, kind barrister. I'll entreat you no more.
By the way, who's in that portrait that hangs by the door?"
"Wa, that's your'r father'r's own father'r, old Angus McCloor."
Now with that response, the younger man swore!

"So that's the old goat who drove my father to sea,
Away from his home to a foreign country!
Where he had to slave in the dawn of his life,
Supporting a young son and a sickly frail wife!

"Instead of the heir to a proud ancient clan,
He lived and worked like the commonest man,
Trying to find a cure for my mother and to educate me,
But she died anyway, and then so did he!

"Yes, on their graves, I solemnly swore,
That they'd be reburied, laird and lady of Castle McCloor!
So that justice could be partially won,
And the pig in the portrait would then be undone!

"Ah, and that must be the cane, as my father had said,
Which caused that jagged scar on the top of Dad's head.
Could those be his bagpipes that I see over there,
Or is it just his fat gut inflated with air?"

"Your'r grandfather played the pipes, I hear'r tell,
But the older ones say he didn't do well."
"Ah, MacLockly, no note could be blown half as sour,
As the face on the wall, so homely and dour!"

Laughing out loudly, he continued his jest.
"How did his face get in with the rest?
We have a great gaping ape in the family tree,
Swinging about like some mascot monkey!"

"Young Philip, I beg ye te take proper car're.
I didn't tell ye those tales just te give ye a scar're!"
But the defiant young laird now stepped forth a firm pace
And threw a goblet of wine in the picture's grim face!

"What puzzles me most, I have to confess,
Is why my dear granny married that mess?
No wonder it took him nearly half of his life,
To find a good woman to be his poor wife!

Philip then noticed MacLockly'd blanched white.
"What's wrong, my fair friend? Did I give you a fright?
The rock of his tomb is not the moor's yielding slime,
No! His bones won't emerge until God ends this time!"

Then the younger man's wrath gave way to dismay.
"I'm sorry, dear friend. I got carried away!
How could I take my wrath out on you
When the ghosts of this place have invaded me too?

"Yeah, when I threw that goblet of wine in his face,
It was almost like he felt the disgrace!
I'd feel no more satisfied if the picture was real!
Come, Mr. MacLockly, how do you feel?"

Then the two men parted to meet the next day.
Each regretted that MacLockly could not lengthen his stay.
Turning on his flashlight, the Scott greeted the night,
While McCloor stood watching till he vanished from sight.

Back into the castle, Philip then turned,
But he wondered greatly about the things he had learned.
He had to venture into those tunnels below,
Where none of these fearful highlanders would go.

Taking his flashlight, he soon found the door,
Which had been locked forty years, maybe more.
It creaked on its hinges; the air became stale,
And it took all of his courage so that his heart would not fail.

Down into the dungeon on stairs of cold stone,
Down to the dungeon completely alone.
Each step that he took made the door grow more small,
Until soon he knew there'd be no door at all.

The bottom of the place had seen no mason's hand,
And the tunnel twisted onward as far as he scanned.
He stopped for a moment in his island of light,
For each side of him was as black as the night.

Bits of dew and cobweb from the ceiling there hung.
By now, all moisture had left McCloor's tongue.
The words of MacLockly now rung in his mind,
What in this lonely tomb would he find?

Once again, the tunnel took another sharp turn.
Ah, for fresh air and light, he now yearned,
For the stale air grew warmer, the hole became hot.
The fear of the place, the young heir now fought.

In a small chamber, he saw now the rack,
With a white-boned skeleton still stretched on his back,
Iron maidens in chains and skeleton frames,
And rusting iron bars once glowing with flames.

Then he noticed small holes carved in the stone walls,
Small little cells, the size of horse stalls.
Into these cells, Philip could not clearly see,
For these iron gates were locked, and he had not the key.

Peering around, he spied one open gate,
But cold fingers of fear called him to wait.
His courage must win; he couldn't relent,
So in an effort of will, forward he went.

Slowly, yes, so slowly, he crawled in that hole,
His stomach now churning, anguish tearing his soul.
But his coat got caught on the bar of the door,
Slamming it shut as from his jacket, it tore.

Then Philip McCloor let out a sharp scream,
It was the worst fate of any bad dream,
With the bones of those prisoners, his would soon rot,
The iron door would not yield any way that he fought.

He started to cry; his limbs began to shake,
From this terrible nightmare, he would never awake.
Trapped in a hole, staring out at his fate,
He was sickly and trembling in a horrible state.

MacLockly would never venture down here, he knew,
Death by starvation must surely ensue.
Sitting there helplessly through iron bars, he then stared,
Praying to God that his life might be spared!

Then in the distance bagpipes, he heard play,
From the source of those tunnels that wind and then sway.
Who was it or what was it that was coming his way?
Producing eerie sounds, he wished he could say.

Then his ears perceived tapping like the tip of a cane.
The throbbing in his head nearly drove him insane.
"Oh, MacLockly, MacLockly, save me from here!"
The bagpipes grew louder, and the tapping more clear.

His heart pounded wildly as if to tear from his chest,
And the sound of the tapping each time it did rest!
He wrenched at those bars which were so firm and quite tight.
Waiting, just waiting, for it to come into light.

Then a breeze seemed to float through that musty dead air,
From that dark passage that lead to the stair.
His head burning with sweat, and his hands were ice-cold.
The grip of the tomb had him in terrors firm hold.

Trapped, he could neither fight nor run for his life.
His throat was so dry; it cut like a knife.
His lungs heaved so hard; he was ready to choke,
And blood trickled down from the nails he had broke.

Nearer, yet nearer, those pipes now did sing,
Through the corridors of death, the tapping did ring.
Stories of MacLockly through his head swiftly did fly,
Shouting, "Philip McCloor, you're now going to die!"

Then through that dark passage, a specter appeared,
With a stout cane in his hand and a red flowing beard,
So Philip knew at once who this had to be,
There came Angus McCloor, none other than he!

In the hold of this terror, Philip gathered his pride,
That old haunt would find no cowardly worm, there inside.
Panic and pride then tore Philip in two,
Yet he was determined of what he must do.

Slowly and directly, the old ghost menacingly neared.
The wine that was thrown, still dripped from his red beard.
From and unknown source, the bagpipes blew high,
Philip could see now some cold light in his eye.

One white hand latched onto the door.
Philip just stared; he could do no more!
With the other hand, the specter drew out a key.
Would he use the rack to produce misery?

As the hand turned the key, the lock gave a click.
McCloor's only hope was that death would come quick.
The ghost beckoned him forth with a look of cold rage
And made ready to speak as Philip crawled from the cage.

"Ye must be moor-re car-refuel in this damn r-rats layer-r.
Ah, don want te lose my son's only heir-r!"
Saying this roughly, he laughed, causing all fear to retire,
And the young heart turned from hate laughed with his grandsire!

Love Poem of a Cad

"My darling, I'd gladly die for thee!"
(If I weren't so busy living for me.)
"Or swim for you the deepest sea"
(In the shallow tanks of imagery.)
"And strive to make you what you want to be."
(As long as I control, you can be free.)

"I'll lay the very world at your feet,"
(Oh, excuse me if I happen to cheat.)
"Yes, on the throne of my heart, you have the seat."
(On the lap of the last girl who thought I was neat.)
"So I'll wrap you up in romance sweet."
(Until someone more desirable, I happen to meet.)

"Beware of those heralds of morality!"
(Listen to them and you might get free!)
"Just abandon yourself in totality,"
(Enabling me to name my own fee.)
"For my love will last quite ultimately."
(As long as it is convenient for me.)

Birth of a Revelation

I have always heard that mankind was fashioned in the image of God,
But still the fact He loves us so has always struck me rather odd.
Thus, I did believe it more in theory than in fact,
Misty, nebulous perceptions forming nothing quite exact.

I was waiting, nervously waiting—why did it take so long?
My wife's condition worsened; things started to go wrong!
They sent me off to wander in the wondering of a waiting room.
Pacing, praying with my coffee cup, as I dared not to presume!

Finally, the awaited messenger beckoned, clad in hospital green,
And wound me through antiseptic passages to yet another scene.
"Your wife is fine—it's a girl!" she said as we traveled down the hall.
So I was to meet my daughter for the very first time of all!

There she was, my Heidi Ho, so tender and so small!
Then welled there up a song in me like none I could recall!
She looked so like my Martha and yet a bit of me
Created in our own images as anyone could see.

So this is something of what it means, why God's love for me!
This is why it can't be earned, but why it's given free!
For He is truly the great Father, and I His little son,
Who, from His great example, teaches me love for my little one.

How could Heidi win my love? Where did her value lie?
After all, what good was she, she could only wet and cry?
All those naughty things she'd do, how could I cherish her dear?
If that question is so absurd, why are sinners lost through fear?

The Gift of Music

In the winter, listen to me of Holland, near Saint Nicholas Day,
'Twas in a simple farmhouse, where a sick boy lay,
His mother had died; the baby had too.
When he would follow, no one ever really knew.

At least in his grandparents' house, he was surrounded by family care,
With always an uncle, aunt, or cousin appearing from somewhere,
To give him the hope to wait for the light,
That brightened his room after long winter's night.

So it was no surprise when his young uncle came in
To smile at the boy with a mischievous grin.
He was lank and long like a bright-copper wire
With eyes of green and hair of fire.

"Ome Jan, do you know what I'd like on Saint Nicholas Day?"
"I don't know, I came the answer with the proper delay.
I'd like a harmonica like yours to play,
So I can make music like you if you show me the way."

How often had young Jan given the boy joy?
When he'd brought out his magical, musical toy,
Producing and amazing heart-lifting tone.
Lingering still when the child lay alone?

So his own instrument, Jan, with great tenderness, laid on the chest
Of the sick little boy who smiled at his guest.
And then Jan hurried off quickly telling the boy to take rest,
Hiding emotions that were fighting hard to crest.

"My poor little one, you'll never live so long,
Not long enough to learn the simplest song."
So thought the uncle praying to be wrong,
As he rushed out the door, the urge to weep was too strong.

But the smile seldom left the little boy's face,
As lie fingered that harmonica, his comforting grace.
So he greeted the Lord in the great promised land,
Still clutching that harmonica tight in his small tender hand.

His uncle never lost his ability to cheer
And the joy he brought to many year after year!
In Holland, then America, with sons of his own,
He'd make the world happier with the harmonica's tone.

For young Uncle Jan became my father, you see,
And when sick as a boy, I shared in that glee!
Which lives on since his death in God's mystery,
Of how love never ends, and so it should be.

And so now that Saint Nicholas and Christmas are near,
If I strain, if I listen, I can nigh hear,
The sounds of harmonicas playing from so far away,
Where a certain uncle and nephew found time to play!

Corcoran's Night Before Christmas

'Twas the night before Christmas and all through the joint,
Not a creature was stirring, 'cause there wasn't no point.
The guards in their towers had polished their guns with great care
In case of a sudden bad inmate scare.

Me and my homey were snug in our cell
When we rose up quickly to see what the hell!
My cellie soon settled back into his bed.
Since he was in the lower, he cracked his fool head.

But being quite conscience, I now slid down
To see some bearded fat-bellied old clown.
I could tell he was northern 'cause he dressed all in red,
And he was singing some song about a reindeer and sled.

Out of his bag, he pulled out all kinds of shit.
And I wondered how in the hell did it all fit.
When suddenly the C.O. made his loud stand,
The stupid old fool had brought contraband!

Like magic, this fatso was through the yard door!
Tearing the red jacket, he so brazenly wore.
His liftoff was swift with the ringing of bells,
Waking the homies all snug in their cells.

He buzzed the yard once before flying up to the sky,
In a sled pulled by reindeer what a hell of a guy!
His voice rang out on this most special of nights,
"I'm outta here, baby! Corcoran, I really bites!"

The Guide

While I sit in pain, so all alone,
On a road so dark and so unknown,
A figure in white takes my hand.
He's leading me, though I can hardly stand.

"Why are we here?" I ask so sad.
"I don't like this place. It feels so bad."
He extends to me a nail-pierced hand.
"Just follow me, child, till you understand."

"It hurts, and it's scary, and I've lost my life!"
"No, my son, you've only lost your wife.
And I have her too, so don't you fret.
I guard your life, and it's not done yet.

"Get up and walk, we've places to go.
I'll wait for you when your going gets slow."
He lifted me back up to my feet,
Where I could stand and our eyes could meet.

The road was foggy; I couldn't steer,
But I looked into His eyes, and they were clear!
Clear enough to help me see,
He knew my road to eternity!

Sequoia's Secret Realm

We gazed upon the meadow—the meadow golden brown.
We climbed upon the trail way—a redwood fallen down.
A father, son, and niece, we wandered from the town,
As sun's once radiant smile turned slowly to a frown.

Our trail a smitten giant; his toes stretched up so high,
They reached the tops of houses, roots planted in the sky!
How could such a mammoth fall? We paused to wonder why.
It served as our bridge today instead of roosts for birds to fly.

Alighting from our fallen host, wooded hills now gently rose,
Filled with his living siblings, looking down in kingly pose,
Flanked here and there by stately pines in uneven rows,
Many burnt or broken by lightning's flashing blows!

We paused to watch some feeding fauns, who wandered from the
    knoll.
Peace and nature's tranquility alighted upon the soul
Watching, listening carefully, nearer to us, they stole.
Winds and plants and creatures fair, making us feel whole.

Then came the rustling from the trees like waves upon the seas,
Whose giant waves of white rushed forth to swallow up those trees.
Then as if by magic's song, those walls fled on running breeze,
For we stood within the clouds, that those winds would tease.

Engulfed by ghostly whiteness in nature's glorious home,
Like wanderers in an enchanted land, we wished no more to roam.
We could hear the movements of the clouds as treetops, they would comb,
And see the whiteness ebb and flow like the sea's own albin foam.

Were we still on planet earth or in some realm surreal?
The mystery of this place so deep that we could keenly feel.
That this was a world sublime where ugliness must kneel,
Bowed down by lovely goodness overpowering, supremely real!

Loath, we were to leave that place of beauty bathed in white,
Where even the growing darkness shed unearthly light!
But fog and storm to travelers are warnings to take flight.
So we crossed back on giant's trail, fleeing the coming night!

We paused upon our woody friend to watch those following faun.
Wandering the boggy meadow till the mist rolled on and on,
Engulfed in growing whiteness until they faded into gone.
Now even within the cloud itself, we were rained upon!

Exiled now by firm edicts of the reigning gale,
We found our cozy van close by, waiting to set sail,
Which whisked us back to our own world, quickly without fail!
Cold and wet but warmed within by memories of our trail.

The Trail of the Owl

A trio on a mission plies Sequoia's own back trails,
Eyes casting downward to where the hawk now sails,
Peering from the lofty heights, where the majestic redwood pales.
Truly a place created for the making of fine tails!

Away from the sunlit cliffs into the shadow's green,
Where the red bark peeks secure from foliage in between.
And the silence of the forest fills that life-filled scene,
That healing born of nothingness, abundant, so serene.

The lass with the raven hair leads confidently the way,
Up twisting tuffs of greenery that host the bears at play,
Until a skittish buck, up front, demands that they delay,
Velvet clad sharp antlers tossed to their dismay!

Carefully they circle and flee the young brown deer.
The guide knows the way around; there's not a thing to fear.
Her dad and her sister follow merrily in the best of cheer.
Before they all know it, they're standing in the clear!

The travelers aren't harried by deer or even bear,
They fearlessly trod faithfully through mosquitoes' ferny lair!
With repellant and with swatting, they take quite rapid care
To move swiftly up and then away from buzzing demons there!

In search of elusive owls that hunt those twilight skies,
To try to spot the spotted owls, now that was the searchers' prize!
For in silence owls, they fleetly fall, and in silence, they arise,
Swiftly sailing through the air on wings soundless in surprise!

From amongst the trees is faintly heard a lonely female's cry,
Filling up the vaulted canopy of the dimming twilight sky.
Foot heavy travelers now revived to spring up feeling spry,
Scramble as the clarion calls beckon from on high!

Heidi, with the flowing hair, like the raven's wing,
Mimicked then the knight in flight, that coming home soon king,
Announcing to his waiting queen his delicacies to bring,
Tasty treats to motivate his expectant bride to sing!

So father and young sister pursued her close behind,
As the mystery of owl's nest was beginning to unwind.
Heidi was directing, and the others were quick to mind.
Elusive nests in the redwoods, they'd surely spring to find!

The signal was quickly given for the group to then advance,
Eagerly awaiting their anticipated chance,
Hoping to spy the queen at each expectant glance,
Like dreamers now enchanted in some fine woodland trance!

Heidi now pulled forth a mouse by its betraying tail
And set it on the fringe near the leafy trail.
Then clicked she so deceptively at the shy female.
From out of the nowhere did the owl queen sail!

Now Rose, the younger sister, with bright and sparkling eye,
Stepped up quite spryly to give the initial try.
Before she even knew it, the queen came speeding by,
Hosting her captive mouse up against the evening sky!

The father, then he tried it, mouse tail firmly in his hand,
A bit more unsteady, unsure just where to stand.
He looked and briefly waited, then totally unplanned.
The male swooped right around him, not stopping first to land.

So in the silent twilight, like arrows loosed of yore,
Soundlessly they wing and turn, undetectably they soar.
They'll swoop within inches as you do nothing but ignore.
Then they'll do the same again as unseen as just before!

Appearing like footballs, caught up by reaching trees,
They soar like gilded eagles; they hunt with greatest ease,
Camouflaged like humble peasants, that no one ever sees,
But feathered monarchs of the skies, they glide on servant breeze!

So even as the twilight gives birth to infant night,
The dinning of the owls is done; the servers take their flight.
Now the daughter known as Heidi leads them home from sylvan site.
Images are on the wing. Everything is more than right!

The Lady of Pine Lake

Outside the wooden cabin, a tiny fire was sparked.
A blackened ring of weathered stones had this place well marked.
Its growing flames illuminates where cars and trucks are parked.
This was the destination for which the lad embarked.

Far from home, he journeyed to meet his father's kin,
To dwell among forgotten trees near the wooded fen.
The night too grand and beauteous to be wasted there within,
So there they sat by the old cabin, nature's very den.

He watched the flame's reflected glare
In his grandfather's steady stare,
A sturdy, full-bearded man with white and silver hair,
Who could be fully present and yet be wandered off somewhere.

Father and son were so different. Shaun had hardly known this man,
For Shaun's father's life was business, so unlike his grandpa, Dan,
As trips and ventures moved Mark by quite a different plan,
Leaving him with just no time to visit with his clan.

So Shaun resolved to come alone to meet his sire's line.
He was bright and strong at eighteen years, so the time was fine,
To acquaint himself with his rural folk, who sat beneath the pine,
Where one could savor this old one's lore like the choicest wine!

For a fortnight now, he wandered trails with his father's sire.
He'd learned about which paths to take, avoiding the meadow's mire.
He'd learned the plants and animals and how to build a fire.
To discover now, the old man's thoughts had transformed into desire.

Surely magic abode within this man, so Shaun's cousins said,
Something more than eye can see but could be sensed instead.
For scholars often overlook what children have quickly read,
Yes, something more about the man than an old gray head.

On one rare visit, as a boy, Shaun could still recall
How Grandpa Dan's cabin seemed filled up wall to wall.
Grandkids, friends, and relatives came there one and all,
Transported off to unknown realms as Grandpa would enthrall!

He spoke of spirits in the woods that others long forgot,
Of chance meetings with unearthly folk, totally unsought,
And how the shadows of the trees evoke some eerie thought,
Revealing things deemed past away that were really not.

So lost in thought, the old man's gaze was fixed upon the flame.
With no coaxing from the younger man, soon the answer came.
"An old man's dreams may take him off, so he's really not to blame,
But to lock you out of my current thought would be an awful shame."

He looked upon the liquid gold that the moon had made.
"I'll tell you now the story of the lady of the Pine Lake."
The old man rose and stretched as one now fresh awake
As he strode out near the shore to watch the small waves break.

"Once a young man came from far away, drawn to this very shore,
In his heart conviction, there really must be more.
Then music played within his heart like the fiddling of a score!
As he opened wide his soul to it, freely did it pour!

"Yet not a fiddler could he see as stars winked as golden eyes,
But the music rose so sweet and fair, he was lost in its surprise!
For there are things the soul must know before the mind denies.
Then saw he dance, a maiden fair, as the notes did rise!

"So lovely and so fair was she that she rapt him there in ecstasy!
Her fluid motions, like the stream, executed gracefully,
But then in one mistaken thought, he questioned this reality,
Of that maiden slim and lithe, enchanted by that tune like he.

"Right then and there, the music quit. He saw the dancer gone!
He felt an emptiness in his heart like one cruelly put upon.
So he waited longingly till the coming of the dawn,
But no more did he spy her dance, graceful as a faun.

"Here upon this very shore, he'd take his stand, peering in the night,
Listening for that elusive tune and that spritely sight.
He'd shun the urge for slumber's arms with redoubled might,
Slowly drifting off, losing the dreamer's fight.

"One night it came, the fiddler's tune! He jumped up to his feet!
He saw the lady dancing there, and their eyes did meet!
Lovely was her countenance, and her voice came crystal sweet.
He found himself dancing toward her in motions deft and fleet!

"Holding forth her moonlit arm to him so invitingly,
She said, 'If you'll have no other, come and dance with me!'
So right here on this shoreline, danced they both so free!
Moved by unseen minstrels in a waltz of mystery.

"Yes, even now upon this shore, I've heard the two still dance!
So listen up with unseen ears, for the fiddlers, just by chance,
To see them in the moonlight, captured by your glance,
Happily captivated like two spirits of romance!"

"Do you yourself believe it?" Shaun asked his aged host.
His grandfather's eyes now glowing like an ember's roast!
"Shaun, you believe, so you must watch at the young man's post,
For you too are filled with magic, even more than most."

Then Shaun heard that tune from the fiddler's bow,
A lovely melody like an ancient river's flow.
Was it real or just imagined? The mind could never know,
Played by unseen fiddlers, whose presence failed to show.

Shaun glanced up, then quick to see the sight that of living lore!
He watched to see the dancers, gliding on the moonlit shore,
For his grandfather and grandmother were dancing there once more,
Just as they had often done in the days of yore!

The Dragon Named Too Much

There beat down on bended knee, the warrior reawakened.
He smelt the stench of dragon's breath and heard its evil croak.
His scarlet eyes transformed as such by cloud of monstrous smoke,
Attacking both his lungs and chest as he struggled not to choke!

His shield-maid stood there by his side with red and blackened skin,
Lithe, strong, armed, and resolute, her strength came from within.
The warrior sensed that with her aid, they must now surely win.
Together they must heal the land of creature's fiery sin!

Bloody was the twosome with the children to defend.
Weary were the knightly twain upon all must depend.
So up he sprang upon the beast. It was time to make an end.
With a raging battle cry, he did the dragon rend!

The blade then found its mark; his lightening aim was true!
Finding there that heartless heart, his blade now ran it through!
The writhing worm in death throws, a final flame he blew.
Heat and pain and flying arm were all the knight now knew!

The maiden slashed, the blood sprayed wide from foul worm's wounded wing.
Just the thing to distract the beast from the fatal sting,
Delivered by our warrior, inspired to catlike spring.
With his valiant lady, he'd slain that loathsome thing.

Finally, would there be sweet peace, a time to find some rest?
Could their children be at play since they passed the test?
Would fair lands heal again from flames fanned from the west?
Now how could fair serenity fail to be their guest?

Knightly eyes reopened to see the monster slain!
At first, he felt exultant joy, but then he felt the pain.
Blood, human red and dragon black, did their venture stain.
He saw her struggle to her feet with an awful strain.

"Come to me and heal me" was all that she could say.
"I am so deeply wounded. T'will be death if I delay!"
But the warrior's wounds were grievous, in his blood he lay.
She dropped her sword by his face and slowly walked away.

Solitary beneath the Stars

He starred into the star-flecked sky,
Bits of brightness sparkled high,
But all he could do is wonder why,
It could never replace her twinkling eye.

The background darkness wove its spell,
Suspended above, a bottomless well.
Alone in thoughts, only his heart could tell,
Into the shadows of silence, there he fell.

Where was she who could stir up light
In the caverns of the night?
What if forever, she'd elude his searching sight?
The cool of the evening kissed the chill of fright.

Where was she who dispels the clouds of gloom,
Whose golden laughter could flood every room?
If emptiness be nothing, as some may presume,
How is joy so nourished as this it consumes?

But where are joy and comfort's arms?
Where can she be with her radiant charms
Beyond the houses or those distant farms?
The unfulfilled heart echoes in hollow alarms.

Not so much as a ghost, she strolls there by his side,
All sensory assurance must now be denied.
The balm of her touch cannot be applied.
To the shifting of winds, his heart will confide.

And so he travels a solitary soul,
His companion, the darkness, fills that deep hole,
Whose only radiance is the shimmer of coal,
Till his eyes spy her approaching him over yonder knoll.

The End or Beginning?

How long and dry this trail has now wound!
Up relentless twists around and around,
No shade or breeze, just dry dusty ground,
No saving breath where hope may be found!

Have you found yourself on a similar way?
Too worn to continue where you just couldn't stay?
Where each breath comes hard and you'll not delay
As the sun beats down in a sizzling ray?

Now we must seek our invisible guide of the trail,
Who has born in us, His will not to fail.
He'll not move aside and will never bail,
Though drained by our weakness, we'll respond as quite hail!

Yes, I say it quite easy, and it is not hard to write,
But believe me when I say that I have passed through that night,
Where despair beats down hope that ought might go right,
Where elusive light stays well hidden from sight!

A fool says in his heart, "There is no God to see,
For if He truly were, then where is He for me?"
In spite of resistance, terrible testings won't flee,
Then springs the voice of our God like waves from the sea!

Hold on! Hold on! My friend, for God is so near,
Through the twisted fog of tired vision, see Him appear!
To justify hope so apparently dead, crushing the reigning deception
  of fear,
Refreshing your heart with His laughter while he dries each tear!

For more than once, I hiked a trail steep, dry and drear,
Longing for waters flowing deep, blue and clear,
On the verge of surrender, though relief was so near,
Provided by the Lord of the trail, ever listening to hear!

Be then not slow to vent your laughter for today!
For no trouble yet born was licensed long to stay.
Begin again to rejoice at the birth of each new day.
Yesterday's death brings again God's renewed array!

This poem, born like my grandson, Davin Zegers, on the fourth of
  July!

About the Author

Born October 13, 1951, in Oxnard, California, into a family of storytellers, it is no wonder that John J. Zegers became one too.

Whenever members of the Zegers family gather in America or in Holland, the stories abound!

There is a rich reservoir of tales coming from the author's father, John, having survived the German occupation of Holland and from his mother, Anna, who crossed the desert coming from Texas to California on splintery plank roads.

Cultural diversity can and did lead to problems, but it also produced a richness of story backgrounds. John himself married a Mexican American girl.

John grew up in Porterville, California, attending St. Anne's Church and grammar school. At age fourteen, he attended Ryan Preparatory Seminary in Fresno, feeling a call to the priesthood. It was there that John was converted from being a poetry hater into a writer and poet himself by the great Jesuit fathers.

After graduating from San Joaquin Memorial High in Fresno, John discerned his vocation lay elsewhere, finding it at age twenty-two, in the Charismatic Renewal. This lead him into youth ministry, including almost thirty-five years in the Youth Recollection Ministry.

Graduating high school, John graduated from Porterville City College.

Before graduating high school, his family took a life-transforming trip for the young poet to meet his father's family in Holland. It was a time of joy and self-discovery!

John and Martha were married April 23, 1977, and raised up their three children. John returned to college, Fresno State, to complete his teaching credential in 1988. This was a time of severe testing, leading to separation and divorce!

His newly acquired position as teacher at Corcoran State Prison was a fulfilling and enriching godsend where he would spend eighteen happy years!

After thirteen years of trials and struggles, John's marriage to Martha was healed, and together, in Tulare, California, they enjoy their children and grandchildren!

CPSIA information can be obtained
at www.ICGtesting.com
Printed in the USA
FSHW021019270221
78996FS

9 781098 052089